He was going to kiss her.

She didn't know how she knew it but she did.

And she was going to let him. Even though she knew without a doubt that she shouldn't.

He came closer.

He leaned in.

She tilted her chin ever so slightly.

And then he did it. He kissed her.

On the cheek.

"Have a good night's sleep," he said as he stepped back.

It took Paris a moment to realize what had happened. A moment in which she just stood there, stunned and a little embarrassed that that tilt of her chin might have let him know she'd expected more.

And no matter how hard she tried, she couldn't seem to stop wishing he would have pulled her into his arms and kissed her until her toes curled and she couldn't remember what day it was.

Dear Reader,

A rewarding part of any woman's life is talking with friends about important issues. Because of this, we've developed the Readers' Ring, a book club that facilitates discussions of love, life and family. Of course, you'll find all of these topics wrapped up in each Silhouette Special Edition novel! Our featured author for this month's Readers' Ring is newcomer Elissa Ambrose. *Journey of the Heart* (#1506) is a poignant story of true love and survival when the odds are against you. This is a five-tissue story you won't be able to put down!

Susan Mallery delights us with another tale from her HOMETOWN HEARTBREAKERS series. *Good Husband Material* (#1501) begins with two star-crossed lovers and an ill-fated wedding. Years later, they realize their love is as strong as ever! Don't wait to pick up *Cattleman's Honor* (#1502), the second book in Pamela Toth's WINCHESTER BRIDES series. In this book, a divorced single mom comes to Colorado to start a new life—and winds up falling into the arms of a rugged rancher. What a way to go!

Victoria Pade begins her new series, BABY TIMES THREE, with a heartfelt look at unexpected romance, in *Her Baby Secret* (#1503)—in which an independent woman wants to have a child, and after a night of wicked passion with a handsome businessman, her wish comes true! You'll see that there's more than one way to start a family in Christine Flynn's *Suddenly Family* (#1504), in which two single parents who are wary of love find it—with each other! And you'll want to learn the facts in *What a Woman Wants* (#1505), by Tori Carrington. In this tantalizing tale, a beautiful widow discovers she's pregnant with her late husband's best friend's baby!

As you can see, we have nights of passion, reunion romances, babies and heart-thumping emotion packed into each of these special stories from Silhouette Special Edition.

Happy reading!

Karen Taylor Richman
Senior Editor

Please address questions and book requests to:
Silhouette Reader Service
U.S.: 3010 Walden Ave., P.O. Box 1325, Buffalo, NY 14269
Canadian: P.O. Box 609, Fort Erie, Ont. L2A 5X3

Her Baby Secret

VICTORIA
PADE

SPECIAL EDITION™

Published by Silhouette Books

America's Publisher of Contemporary Romance

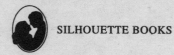 **SILHOUETTE BOOKS**

ISBN 0-373-24503-3

HER BABY SECRET

Copyright © 2002 by Victoria Pade

Visit Silhouette at www.eHarlequin.com

Printed in U.S.A.

Books by Victoria Pade

*A Ranching Family
†Baby Times Three

VICTORIA PADE

is a bestselling author of both historical and contemporary romance fiction, and mother of two energetic daughters, Cori and Erin. Although she enjoys her chosen career as a novelist, she occasionally laments that she has never traveled farther from her Colorado home than Disneyland, instead she spends all her spare time plugging away at her computer. She takes breaks from writing by indulging in her favorite hobby—eating chocolate.

Dear Reader,

Welcome to the first book in the BABY TIMES THREE series about the Tarlington brothers—Ethan, Aiden and Devon—three very different men and their reactions to fatherhood.

Ethan is a computer software magnate who, with the exception of one night of wild, abandoned passion, has put work before any personal pursuits. But those plans change when he finds himself with a dimpled daughter and the one woman who can make him forget all about work.

Aiden is a doctor in the wilderness of Alaska who literally finds a baby boy left on his doorstep—just after he's met the woman who holds his entire town's medical future in the palm of her hand and wiggles her way into his heart.

And Devon…well, Devon is a wildlife photographer and just a bit of a bad boy. About the last thing he ever thought would happen was to find out he's a dad. Not to mention that he might be falling in love with the bearer of that news.

I had a lot of fun opening up these guys' eyes to wonderful women and adorable babies. I hope you'll enjoy reading about them as much as I enjoyed writing about them. Look for Aiden's and Devon's books in the months to come.

All the best,

Victoria Pade

Chapter One

Paris Hanley recognized the voice the minute she heard it. A baritone as deep and rich as Dutch cocoa.

It was coming from the family room of the house she shared with her mother and her daughter, Hannah, and it made Paris forget all about shucking the shoes she'd been dying to get off her aching feet the minute she walked in the door. It made her follow the sound of that distinctive voice in a rush.

"There she is!" her mother exclaimed when Paris burst through the archway of the family room. Then, to Paris, she said, "Look who's here."

Paris had been right. There, with Janine Hanley, sat Ethan Tarlington.

But his presence didn't please her as much as it seemed to please her mother.

"Hi," he greeted.

"Hello," Paris responded without a bit of warmth.

The coolness was uncalled for. He hadn't done anything wrong. In fact, he'd done everything as right as he possibly could have. It was just that she wasn't proud of what she'd let happen between them the one and only other time they'd been together. And the fact that it had served her purposes only complicated things.

So she amended her tone to one of curiosity even as she put herself between Ethan Tarlington and the playpen where her five-month-old daughter was peacefully napping.

"This is a surprise," she said then.

"I knew it would be," her mother said, even though Paris hadn't intended the comment for her. "Imagine the man from the picture showing up on our doorstep. Of course, I wouldn't have let him in if I hadn't recognized him from the snapshot, but since I did I thought you'd be glad to see him again."

The snapshot.

The instant snapshot that Paris had taken when she was supposed to be taking pictures of the tables for the caterer's portfolio and Ethan Tarlington had somehow found his way into the viewfinder instead.

The snapshot she'd pocketed for no reason she'd understood and kept in her sweater drawer ever since. In her sweater drawer where her mother had happened upon it and come to her own false conclusions about Paris having some kind of crush on him.

"Well, I have things to do, so I'll leave you two to talk," Janine said then, getting up from the wicker chair that faced the identical one Ethan Tarlington was sitting in.

Paris wanted to tell her mother to take Hannah with her but she was afraid of drawing too much attention to the baby. In fact, it occurred to her that standing where she was, nearly hovering over the playpen, might do the same thing, so she moved to sit in the seat her mother had vacated.

"Ick, you smell like sausage," Janine said with a laugh as their paths crossed.

"That's what I've been demo-ing all day."

"At the grocery store," Ethan Tarlington contributed. "Your mother told me you're still doing odd jobs so you can paint."

"Yes, I am."

Janine bid them a general goodbye and left, and for the first time since Paris had come into the room she let her gaze settle directly on Ethan Tarlington.

Either he'd gotten even better-looking or the snapshot and her memory of him hadn't done him justice because it struck Paris all over again how devastatingly handsome he was.

Hair the color of espresso, which he wore devil-may-care longer on top than on the sides or back and finger-combed to perfection. Cerulean-blue eyes so striking, so piercing, they hardly seemed real. A nose that was just hawkish enough to give him character and distinction. Chiseled cheekbones and a jawline so sharp it could slice bread. Lips that managed to be thin and sensuous at once. Broad shoulders and the body to go with them on legs that she knew would elevate him to a full six-four if he were standing.

The perfect specimen.

But that was the last thing she should be thinking about.

So she tried not to, put a businesslike tone into her voice and said, "This really is a surprise."

"Not one you sound too happy about," he said with an arch of well-shaped eyebrows.

No, she *wasn't* happy about seeing him again. But she couldn't say that so she didn't say anything at all.

"Cinderella is supposed to be thrilled to see the prince, isn't she?" he added into the brief silence she left. "Or don't I fit that bill?"

Oh, he fit it, all right. At least, he would have under different circumstances.

"I don't think that I'm a likely Cinderella."

"We met at the ball, spent the evening together and you disappeared into thin air. Isn't that Cinderella?"

Except the *ball* had been a Denver-area charity dinner in his honor and she hadn't been there as a guest all dolled up in a fairy godmother's gift of gown and slippers. She'd been hired by the caterer as a cocktail waitress and she'd been wearing black trousers and a tuxedo shirt.

And she hadn't disappeared at the respectable stroke of midnight...

"I tried to find you before this," Ethan Tarlington continued. "For that whole next week afterward. But you aren't listed in the phone book and you didn't leave me even an e-mail address. The caterer wouldn't give me any information about you—in case I was a stalker, I guess. Plus you didn't really tell me anything about yourself except that you were a struggling artist. When I called several galleries and finally found someone who had heard of you, she wouldn't tell me anything, either, because she was angling to be the middleman if I was interested in buying some of your work. Then I ran out of time and—"

"Left the country—you told me you were going to. And that you didn't know when you'd be back. That made it seem unlikely that there would be a second…date."

"Still, I thought we hit it off."

"It was a nice enough night," was all Paris would concede. Then she said, "How did you find me now?"

"It was fate. I was flying home last week, reading magazines on the plane, and I hit an article about up-and-coming young artists in the Denver area. Since I'd met one of those—namely you—I read the article and there you were. So I thought, why not give it another try? I called the magazine, talked to the writer, and here I am—looking you up."

"Ah."

Maybe fate was paying her back.

"What snapshot was your mother talking about?" Ethan Tarlington asked then.

"It was one of several I took for the caterer that night. The kind that develop within a few minutes. I caught you by mistake and it wasn't a very good shot of the table setting so I stuck it in my pocket and just happened to bring it home with me.''

Okay, so that was partially untrue. She could easily have altered her view before she took the picture, but she wasn't really sure why she hadn't, and she wasn't going to tell him that any more than she was going to let him know she'd hung on to it all this time.

Besides, she didn't want to talk about that night so she changed the subject. ''Did everything go the way you'd planned overseas?''

''It took longer than I thought it would, but, yes, I did what I set out to do. I opened offices in London, Paris, Amsterdam, Geneva, Hong Kong and Brisbane for Tarlington Integrated Business and Government Software.''

''So you're worldwide. Congratulations.''

''Thanks,'' he said without conceit. But then, that was one of the things she'd liked about him when she'd met him—his ego was not proportional to his reputation, status or megamillion-dollar net worth as one of the stars in the computer software industry.

It seemed to be his turn to change the subject. ''Looks like you've been pretty busy yourself,'' he said with a nod in the direction of the playpen. ''A baby by artificial insemination, according to your mother.''

Paris couldn't keep from grimacing at that. ''She told you?''

''She said you had some female problems and couldn't wait around for Mr. Right.''

The details were even worse. How could her mother have blabbed about her health problems, too?

"My mother talks too much."

"Hannah is a beautiful baby, though."

"You saw her? I mean, was she awake when you got here?"

"Awake and cooing and smiling at me like an angel."

That was not good news to Paris.

But what was done was done and there wasn't anything she could do about it now, so instead she decided to try for a little damage control by cutting this visit short.

"I'm afraid that angel has a doctor's appointment I need to get her to," she lied. "I don't mean to be rude but—"

"Is she sick?"

"No, it's just a well-baby checkup."

"I see."

But he didn't get up to go. Instead he turned his head to look at the playpen again for a long moment.

Then he focused on Paris again and said, "Your mom is a nice lady. Talkative."

"I suppose she is." Paris wondered why he'd started that rather than taking her invitation to leave.

"She told me some things about what's going on with you now."

A wave of panic washed through Paris until she remembered that her mother couldn't tell what she didn't know. But still, she was curious about what he meant so she said, "And what exactly did my talkative mother have to say about me?"

"That it was harder for you to make ends meet with the baby and that you really need money for a new car—which was why you were handing out food samples at the grocery store."

"And she probably made me sound like a martyr or something when she said it, too," Paris said with a small laugh to downplay her mother's report. "My being a single parent by choice is something she's had a hard time grasping."

"Maybe. But she's proud of you. And she's crazy about Hannah."

"Hannah is the light of her life."

"What she said got me to thinking while I've been here, though, and there might be a job you could do for me."

"Do you have sausages that need demonstrating?"

She had absolutely not intended that to sound suggestive in any way. But somehow that's how it had come out.

And it hadn't escaped Ethan Tarlington because his sensuous mouth stretched into a slow smile. A slow smile she remembered all too well.

"No, no sausage demonstrations," he said with a hint of innuendo in his tone, too. "But you do temporary work and that's what this is. Every year I throw a formal dinner party for the people who live in the town where my brothers and I grew up. Dunbar—it's out on the eastern plains, just before Limon. A small town. Not many people this close to Denver have heard of it."

"I haven't."

"Well, anyway, the party takes a lot of preparation

and organization, and since I like to relax and catch up with old friends while I'm there I need someone else to oversee everything. It's a week from tomorrow—next Saturday night—and it's the last-minute things that can bog me down. So what if you came along to Dunbar to do it for me? There's no hotel or motel, but I'll put you up in my house, and for that single week's work I'll pay you enough to buy a new car outright.''

"You're kidding."

"I'm not. It isn't the reason I looked you up, but since things seem to have changed and we're both in need, we'd both come out ahead.''

Her need was clearly greater than his. Which made for quite a dilemma suddenly.

Her mother had been right about the fact that since she'd had Hannah it had been more and more difficult to make ends meet selling the occasional painting and doing odd jobs. And just since Hannah's birth her old clunker of a car had broken down three times, one of them stranding the two of them on a miserably cold, rainy night just two weeks before. The incident had left Paris worried every time she took Hannah out in it now.

The mechanic had left no question that the car had to be replaced, but without steady employment she hadn't been able to qualify for either a loan or a lease on anything else. And she honestly didn't know what to do about it.

Except that now, sitting only a few feet away from her, was a solution.

It was just that that solution was Ethan Tarlington. The man she'd counted on never seeing again.

"I don't have anyone to leave Hannah with," she said suddenly. "My mother is the only person I feel comfortable leaving her with for a whole week, and she's going to Florida tomorrow to visit her sister."

"I know, she told me."

What *hadn't* she told him?

"But that's not a problem," Ethan assured her. "The house in Dunbar is big enough to get lost in so there's plenty of room for Hannah, too. Most of what you'll do can be done with her right by your side, but if it can't, there'll be someone to stay with her because there's a live-in staff of three, plus both of my brothers will be there."

He leaned slightly forward and added in a confidential tone, "That also means five chaperones, in case that makes you feel any better."

It didn't.

But Paris found herself considering his offer in spite of that.

The thought just kept going through her mind that he was only talking about one week. A single week's work that would net her enough money to replace her car.

How much time would Ethan really be spending with her or Hannah, anyway? she reasoned. He was hiring her to free himself to see his friends. Didn't that mean that she would merely be part of the staff and that he wouldn't be giving her or her daughter a second glance?

It seemed likely. More than likely.

And then she could buy a new, safe car…

"If I do this I want it clear that what happened between us before is not going to happen again. I'll be working for you and that's all. Strictly business."

"Strictly business," he agreed without hesitation.

Something about the speed of that concession stung her, though. She didn't understand it, and while she was examining her reaction he seemed to consider the matter settled and stood.

But rather than heading for the front of the house to leave, he surprised her yet again by going to the playpen.

That stopped Paris's examination of her feelings instantly as she nearly jumped to her feet to follow him like a protective mother bear.

"Still snoozing," he said softly, peering into the playpen.

"She's a sound sleeper. She probably won't wake up until I get her to the doctor's office," Paris said to restate her earlier claim of an appointment so that he really might leave.

"Guess I won't be able to say goodbye to her, then."

"No, I guess not."

But he still stood there for another long moment, watching the baby sleep. And giving Paris second thoughts about accepting his job offer.

But it was for Hannah's sake, she reminded herself. The new car she would get out of it was for Hannah's safety.

Then Ethan Tarlington finally broke off his scrutiny of her daughter and headed out of the family room.

"So you'll take the job in Dunbar?" he said along the way.

Again Paris had doubts.

But again she also had to consider the benefits, and choose those over the risks.

"Yes, I'll take the job."

"Strictly business," he reminded, as if he could tell she'd wanted him to.

"Strictly business," she confirmed.

"Okay, then, I'll pick you up at nine Monday morning."

"Maybe it would be better if Hannah and I got there on our own. Is there a bus or train or something?"

"There's a bus that runs from Denver and back but I don't know what the schedule is. And if you drive in with me you'll get there in time to go right to work."

And he was the boss, so what was she going to say to that?

"Nine o'clock Monday morning it is, then, I guess."

They'd reached the door and Paris opened it for him, hoping he wouldn't linger any longer than he already had.

But her hopes were for naught because that's just what he did. Lingering to take a slow, concentrated look at her, his azure eyes going from the top of her short spiky brown hair to her still-aching toes and back again.

"You don't look like a woman who was pregnant

only five months ago. You look great. Even better than I remembered.''

Paris hated how much that pleased her. ''I was careful during the pregnancy. I ate a lot of fruits and vegetables so I didn't gain too much more than baby weight. It went away not long after Hannah was born.''

And why was she telling him that, when she should have been telling him the whole subject was not something an employer and an employee had any reason to be discussing?

''Will there be a uniform I'll need to wear?'' she asked then, as if that were the only reason she could think of for him to say anything about her appearance. And to cover her own unwelcome response to his compliment.

''No, no uniform. You can wear your regular clothes. I was just appreciating the postnatal you is all,'' he said with another of those smiles that were one of the reasons she'd let him sweep her off her feet that other time they'd met.

But she had a lot at stake now and she was determined not to lose sight of that. So she raised a prudish chin to him and said, ''Strictly business.''

''Strictly business,'' he agreed again, just as quickly as the first time.

And like the first time, it stung once more.

Then he said, ''Have a nice weekend,'' and stepped out onto the porch.

''Thanks,'' she responded just before she closed the door behind him and deflated against it.

And that was when it occurred to her why Ethan Tarlington had been so eager to keep things between them strictly business.

It was because of Hannah.

After all, hadn't he said that first night that he wasn't ready for marriage and kids? That they weren't on his near horizon?

He had. And she hadn't doubted for a minute that he'd meant it.

Plus he'd originally "looked her up" because he'd thought they had "hit it off" and he wanted to see her again, yet somewhere along the way he'd obviously gone from wanting to see her again to just wanting her to work for him.

Hannah. It had to be Hannah who had changed things.

But that was okay. It was better than okay, it was for the best.

Because if Ethan Tarlington didn't want to date someone with a child he would keep his distance. He would relegate her completely to the role of employee while he went on about his business.

And that was a good thing. It was just what she wanted.

Except that if it was just what she wanted, why did it sting the same way his eager agreements to keep things strictly business between them had?

She hated to admit it, but this time when she explored her own feelings she realized that it was disappointing that he didn't want her. Child or no child.

But it *was* for the best, she told herself firmly. Because as long as Ethan Tarlington didn't want her, as long as he saw her as nothing more than an employee, as long as he stayed away from her and away from Hannah, he could remain oblivious to the fact that Hannah was his daughter.

And that was just how Paris wanted it.

Chapter Two

Saturday and Sunday had passed more slowly for Ethan than any weekend he could remember. He hadn't been able to concentrate on work. He hadn't been interested in play. He'd had trouble sleeping. And nothing he'd eaten had tasted good.

It wasn't hard to figure out why, when the same thoughts had been going through his mind since the minute he'd left Paris Hanley's house on Friday. The same thoughts that were still going through his mind Monday morning as he had his coffee.

The thoughts all started the same way. At the beginning. The night he'd met Paris.

He'd liked her almost immediately. It hadn't mattered that she was a waitress in a room full of attorneys, executives, financial and computer wizards. It had only mattered that she hadn't fallen all over herself trying to impress him, suck up to him or seduce him. That she hadn't put on any pretenses, any airs.

Plus the way she looked certainly hadn't hurt.

She was a compact little thing. Only about five feet four inches of tight rear end and flat stomach. Of legs that were long despite her height. Of breasts that were just big enough to make a man look twice.

He'd liked the way her short, chestnut-colored hair had a slightly wild air about it in the flipped ends in back and the wisps here and there at the sides and top. It was carefree and cute.

But it framed a face that was more than that.

She had incredible bone structure and skin that was nothing less than luminous. Her mouth was sultry with full lips that old movie magazines would have called kissable. Her nose was an artwork all its own. And then there were her eyes. Eyes with long, thick lashes.

They were actually a pale silver. Not blue. Not gray. But a remarkable, radiant combination of the two that had left him mesmerized the moment he'd looked into them that night.

Mesmerized.

It was still hard for him to believe. Being that awestruck by anyone was an experience he'd never had before, and he'd found himself not caring anymore about the award he'd been receiving. Not caring about any of the other people he was with. Not caring about anything but getting the woman alone so he could have her all to himself.

But that hadn't been easy. She wasn't supposed to

fraternize with the guests, she'd told him. And she'd seemed determined to abide by the rules.

But he'd been more determined to break them. Driven almost.

So he'd kept at her and kept at her.

It had taken him all evening to get her to warm up to him and long after the number of partygoers had dwindled to convince her to have a late dinner with him.

A late dinner at a chic bistro he'd persuaded to stay open just for them. Followed by a walk through the gardens around his house. Then a nightcap in the formal living room so she could see his original Matisse. And then, when one thing led to another...

Wow.

Ethan had relived that encounter in his mind so many times he'd lost count. And it still had the power to rock him even as he sat at his kitchen table on a Monday morning.

Okay, so, no, they hadn't gotten to know much about each other outside the bedroom. A few surface facts mingled with all the flirting and teasing and the palpable sexual attraction. But he hadn't thought that would matter because even though he'd been on the verge of leaving the country, he'd felt as if there would be time after that night to get into the nuts and bolts of things.

But then she'd disappeared.

She was gone when he'd awakened the next morning. Without having said goodbye. Without so much as scrawling her phone number in lipstick on the bathroom mirror. She was just gone. Like Cinderella.

Except she hadn't lost her glass slipper on the way, and he hadn't had only a small kingdom to search for her.

And then he'd had to leave, too, before he'd been able to find her.

Over the months away he'd tried to tell himself to chalk it up to a one-night stand and forget about her.

But that had been easier said than done.

Even when he was so swamped with work that he could hardly see straight, even with no shortage of women willing to keep him company when he wasn't, Paris Hanley had still popped into his thoughts again and again and again.

But the longer he'd been out of the country, the less likely it had seemed that they'd ever reconnect. And he *had* been out of the country for a long time.

The trip he'd initially intended to last six months had stretched to eight. Then ten. Then a full year. Then two months more. And even though Paris Hanley had still been on his mind he'd come to think that too much time had passed, that he'd never see her again. That that single mind-boggling night they'd had together was destined to be the only one and that he would just have to savor the memory that he knew would still be putting a secret smile on his face when he was old and infirm.

And then he'd seen that magazine article on the plane. Complete with a picture that had captured those eyes of hers. Reminding him just how beautiful she was. Reigniting the urge to see her again. Nudging him to try once more to find her.

Fate. When he'd actually managed to persuade the

article's author to give him enough information to track her down—on top of the happenstance of seeing the article in the first place—he'd figured it was fate telling him something.

It was just that now, as he poured his second cup of coffee, he couldn't help wondering exactly *what* fate might have been telling him.

Because now there was Hannah, too.

And that fact was what he'd been going over and over in his mind all weekend as much as thoughts of Paris.

Janine Hanley had been carrying the baby on her hip when she'd answered the door on Friday afternoon. Once the older woman had recognized him from some photograph she'd said her daughter had of him and decided to let him in to wait for Paris's return from work, it hadn't been a big jump for Janine to introduce Hannah to him.

And from there the doting grandmother had been more than willing to tell him all about the baby.

Hannah was five months old.

"I didn't know Paris was involved with anyone," he'd said to Janine as the wheels in his head had begun to turn.

That was when Janine had told him about Paris having some kind of female problem that had thrust her into a now-or-never situation if she wanted to have a child.

"And since she wasn't married or in a relationship, she had artificial insemination," Janine had said.

Artificial insemination.

Ethan hadn't doubted for a minute that Janine Hanley believed that.

But he hadn't found it quite so easy to buy.

Not when Hannah just happened to have been born almost nine months to the day after the night he and Paris had spent together.

Janine Hanley hadn't seemed to know anything about that night, but as she went on talking Ethan had taken a closer look at the baby.

Maybe he was wrong. But Hannah's eyes were remarkable, too. Only not in the same way her mother's were.

In fact, they weren't anything like her mother's eyes.

They were a vibrant aquamarine blue.

Like *his* mother's eyes.

Ethan caught himself staring at the tile floor, picturing Paris in his mind. Picturing Hannah...

Curiosity was eating him up inside.

Was it possible that Hannah was his child?

It certainly seemed possible.

The timing was right. The artificial insemination story could be bogus even if the female problems weren't. And there was the unusual eye color.

But if Hannah was his child, why hadn't Paris said something?

Even though he'd left the country, she could still have tracked him down through his company when she'd found out she was pregnant. And barring that, she could have told him on Friday.

But not only hadn't she, he'd had the sense that she was sorry he'd been anywhere near Hannah. That she was trying to run interference to keep him away from the baby altogether.

But if Hannah was his child why *wouldn't* Paris want him to know? That was the part that most made him doubt his paternity.

Too many other women he knew would have been beating a path to his door for child support. And Paris needed the money more than anyone.

Of course, nothing else about her was like other women, so why should that be? But still he'd had women—okay, one woman in particular—who had gone to great lengths to get all she could out of him for far less reason, and she hadn't been handing out sausages at a supermarket to make ends meet or driving an old junk heap of a car.

So maybe Hannah really was the product of artificial insemination, and the similarity between her aquamarine eyes and his mother's aquamarine eyes was purely a coincidence.

Or maybe one of his brothers had donated sperm to a sperm bank at some point and he just didn't know about it.

"I wouldn't give very good odds on that one," he muttered to himself as he took his coffee cup to the sink.

But his brothers *did* play a role in his reason for that job offer he'd made Paris.

He wanted them to get a look at Hannah, too. To see if they saw in her what he saw in her. To know what they thought.

And maybe in the process he'd be able to figure out what could possibly be going on with Paris to make her keep the fact of his own child from him if Hannah *was* his.

But either way, one thing was certain: he was going to get to the bottom of this.

He clasped the edge of the countertop with both hands and leaned forward, hanging his head as he shook it from side to side.

What a mess this could all be, he thought.

He just hoped that whatever it was that was going on with Paris wasn't what it looked like.

Because what it looked like was that she'd had his baby and kept the news from him.

And that deceit—*any* deceit—was a very big deal to him. Deceitful women were women he didn't want anything to do with. Women he'd vowed to be on the lookout for. And if Paris Hanley was one of those women they had a problem.

If Paris Hanley was one of those women *and* she was the mother of his child they had an even bigger problem.

But he was reserving judgment until he knew the facts.

And keeping his fingers crossed that the facts wouldn't prove the worst.

Because baby or no baby, there was some inexplicable something about Paris Hanley that flipped a switch in him.

And when that switch was flipped it was as if he came alive in a way he never had with any other woman. In a way he never had in his whole life.

And he wasn't sure what that would mean to him

if he discovered she was keeping a secret as enormous as a child of his own making.

Paris hoped none of her neighbors were around to see the limousine that pulled up in front of her house at exactly nine o'clock in the morning. It would cause no end of talk and she didn't relish being the subject of it. At least, she didn't relish being the subject of neighborhood gossip any more than she already had been as the resident unwed mother who everyone believed had been artificially inseminated.

Luckily she had everything packed and ready to go. Including Hannah, who was soundly napping in her car seat. A baby blanket draped over it to keep out the August sunshine and Ethan Tarlington's prying eyes.

He did look wonderful as he got out of the car and came up to her open front door, though—casual and comfortable in khaki slacks and a garnet-colored polo shirt that hugged his broad shoulders and sculpted chest.

Not that the way he looked mattered to her. She was just glad to see that she wasn't underdressed by comparison since she hadn't been sure what to wear. She'd opted for a pair of navy-blue linen drawstring pants and a white split-V-necked T-shirt tucked into them, and it helped that the outfit had been the right choice.

Or at least she told herself that was the only reason watching Ethan approach the house brought her pleasure.

The limousine driver followed him to her door as

Paris slid her suitcase and the smaller one for Hannah out onto the porch.

"Morning," she said perfunctorily.

"Hi," Ethan greeted, much as he had on Friday afternoon.

"I'm all set," she added, turning back inside to sling her purse and diaper bag over her shoulder and pick up the car seat by its handle.

But Ethan didn't let her hang on to the car seat for long. He took it from her with a simple "Let me get this."

As his driver took the suitcases to the limo's trunk, Ethan peeked under the baby blanket canopy. "Is she sleeping again?"

"Morning nap time," Paris confirmed, repositioning the blanket to block his view.

Once she'd locked the front door, she and Ethan followed the driver to the car. The rear door had been left open, and inside Paris could see two rows of seats facing each other. Ethan set the carrier on the backward-facing seat.

"Is there a special trick to this thing?" he asked as he did.

"I need to do it," Paris answered, glad to take over.

Ethan ducked out of the car and freed the way for her to climb in.

She deposited her purse and diaper bag on the roomy floor while she used the seat belts to secure the carrier. It was a whole lot easier job in the limousine than it was in her car. Her car only had two doors, and getting the carrier and herself into the back seat required contortions.

But she was extremely aware that while doing it in the expansive limo might be more convenient, it also had her bending over and giving Ethan a bull's-eye view of her derriere. Which she didn't appreciate.

There was nothing to be done about it, however, so she just buckled the baby carrier in as quickly as she could and then sat beside it, leaving the opposite seat free for Ethan.

"All set?" he asked from the sidewalk.

"All set."

He joined them, then, closing the door behind him rather than waiting for the driver to do it. When he'd settled in he pointed to his left, pushed a button and out came a fully equipped bar. "Would you like something to drink? Coffee? Tea? Soda?"

"I'm fine, thanks."

Another push of the button and the bar disappeared, just as the engine purred to life and the limo moved away from the curb.

The car seemed to glide into motion so quietly, so smoothly, it was as if they were floating. Paris was thrilled with that. It meant Hannah would likely sleep all the way to their destination, and that was exactly what Paris wanted.

"How far is it to Dunbar?" she asked then.

"About 150 miles. It'll take a while."

Too long a while, Paris thought as she realized she was going to spend that entire time one-on-one with

Ethan Tarlington and those blue eyes of his that seemed to be studying her.

She was wondering what to talk about to distract him, when he said, "The drive will give us a chance to get to know a little about each other."

"Like a job interview?"

"I think we're beyond that, don't you?"

Paris wasn't happy about any reference to the intimacy they'd shared fourteen months before but she tried not to show it.

"I'd really like to know about your health problems," Ethan said. "They must have been pretty severe to push you into doing something as extreme as artificial insemination."

The last thing she wanted to talk about with Ethan Tarlington was her health problems. But it occurred to her that telling him what he wanted to know might reinforce her claim that Hannah was the product of artificial insemination, and for the sake of that she decided to allow the conversation.

"I guess any artificial means of having a baby does seem extreme from the outside looking in. But for me it was just a solution. I was diagnosed with endometriosis and cystic ovaries so bad that the first doctor I saw wanted to do a hysterectomy."

"I'm not sure what endometriosis and cystic ovaries are, but they sound serious."

"Female problems," she repeated to simplify, leaving it at that because she didn't want to go into a lecture about uterine lining traveling through her abdominal cavity to attach itself and cause miserable pain and cramping, or about the monthly development of cysts from which ovulation occurred and the problems that developed when those cysts didn't spontaneously dissolve every month the way they were supposed to.

But apparently he was satisfied with her simplification because rather than asking for details, he said, "The *first* doctor—I assume that means you saw others?"

"I wanted kids, not a hysterectomy at twenty-eight. So yes, I got a second opinion."

"And how did that stack up against the first?"

"It was pretty much the same. But the second doctor understood that I wanted to try to have at least one baby before I did anything as final as surgery."

The truth was that having kids had been something Paris had wanted for as long as she could remember and the thought of being denied that was a devastating blow to her. She'd ended up sobbing in the second doctor's office.

"Anyway," she continued, "the second doctor made it clear that having a baby was a now-or-never proposition. If it wasn't already too late. And since I'd just come out of a relationship and there weren't any immediate candidates for husband or father, I looked into artificial insemination."

That was true, too. She *had* looked into it and discovered that it was expensive. So expensive that she'd been terrified that what little window of opportunity she might have would be closed by the time she could save enough money to do it.

Which was when Ethan Tarlington had come along.

That night was vivid in Paris's memory.

Yes, she'd noticed the incredible-looking guest of honor when he'd entered the banquet room, but the last thing she'd been thinking about was having him father her child. Doing a good job and being able to put the evening's pay into her artificial insemination fund was more what was on her mind.

Then he'd started to flirt with her. To tease her. To go all-out in persuading her to see him later on.

He'd been so persistent. So amazingly handsome. So charming and funny. He'd just worn down her defenses until she'd finally given in to having dinner with him. *Just* to having dinner with him.

Certainly making babies with him had not been a consideration. The furthest thing from it, in fact. After all, she'd only slept with one man before that, and it certainly hadn't been on her first date with him. She rarely even kissed on a first date.

But what a date that night with Ethan had turned out to be!

It was like no other date she'd ever been on. Not even with Jason.

Hours had gone by like mere moments. Ethan had made her laugh. He'd been able to talk about art with her more comprehensively than most art professors. He'd paid attention to everything she'd had to say. He'd made her feel as if she were the only woman in the world. And he'd been a perfect gentleman.

Even when he'd finally kissed her it had felt long overdue, and she'd been dying for him to.

Of course it hadn't hurt that by then they'd finished an entire bottle of champagne. But still, the man could kiss. Plus he had a way of holding her, a way no one had ever held her before, that was arousing all on its own. It was as if she could feel the power in his arms, in his muscular body. A primitive, masculine power, leashed into a gentleness that made her feel safe, protected, cherished.

And very turned on.

So turned on that she had wanted to stay kissing him forever. She'd wanted to stay held in his arms forever.

But more than that, she'd wanted to feel his touch, too. His hands on her body…

"I didn't know you were having health problems that night."

"I wasn't," she said. "I mean, I was, but I felt fine that night." And this was where she had to begin the lies. "The appointment with the first doctor was on that Monday after we were together. That was when I got the bad news. I saw the second doctor on that Thursday and everything went fast from there."

She hated lying. To him or to anyone else. But she'd decided that if she was going to be with him for the next week, if Hannah was going to be around him, she would say anything she had to, to throw him off the track.

"You must have had artificial insemination right away."

"Right away. Within two weeks of when we met," she confirmed. "And then Hannah was born early." Only four days early, but Paris didn't offer that little detail.

"So that night we were together—"

"Was just a moment out of time before I got the worst news of my life and had to find a way to deal with it."

A moment during which she'd discovered in herself such a strong urge to have him make love to her that she hadn't been able to resist it.

She'd wanted it as badly as if they'd been together for months. As if there had been a prolonged mounting of sexual tension that had culminated on that night in a need so demanding it had to be satisfied.

Then—and only then—had baby making come to mind for her.

Not as a driving force, by any means. Not as the reason she was with Ethan. Not as the reason she wanted him. Not as a calculated act. Just as a little whisper in the back of her mind that told her she was likely ovulating. That here was a handsome, successful, intelligent, creative, personable man who was a better candidate for fathering her child than anyone she would ever find in a sperm bank's catalog.

And so she'd done what she'd never done before. She'd thrown caution to the wind and spent the remainder of the night in bed with Ethan Tarlington.

"It *was* a moment out of time, wasn't it?" he repeated as if she'd struck a chord with that phrase, smiling as if he were remembering just how good that moment had been.

That moment that had culminated not only in the most incredible lovemaking she'd ever experienced, but as a moment out of time that had given her her heart's desire when she'd needed it most. Because astonishingly, she'd gotten pregnant from that single night with him.

She thought her lies about the timing must have appeased whatever it was that had been going through his mind, because Ethan returned to the earlier part of the conversation. "Didn't artificial insemination seem...I don't know, impersonal? Clinical?"

"Of course there's that element to it. But there are advantages, too."

"For instance?"

"For instance, a baby by artificial insemination belongs only to that baby's mother. And that mother is free to raise that baby as she sees fit, without any interference." And without anyone being able to demand custody of the child and take the child away from that mother.

"You don't think it's a problem that Hannah doesn't have a dad?"

"There are a lot of kids raised in single-parent homes. I was. I think what's important is that the parent she has is devoted to her. That I'm determined to be the best parent I can be. And that I love her as much as any two parents possibly could."

Ethan nodded as if he understood, but was still not convinced that was preferable to a traditional family.

He let it drop, though, and said, "And you don't have any idea who the father is?"

Again she answered in general rather than specifically. "In artificial insemination there's complete anonymity. The woman is given the donor's physical description but no picture. She knows his occupation, his educational background, his health history and the health history of his family. But that's all. The man himself is known only by number."

"And basically rendered obsolete."

"I don't think anything is ever going to make men obsolete," she assured. "I'm actually grateful to the man who gave me Hannah. I feel as if he did something wonderful and extremely generous for me when I needed it most."

Ethan raised his chin in what looked like acknowledgment of that.

"What will you tell her when she asks about her father?" he asked then.

"Now *that* one I haven't come up with an answer for yet."

"No, I don't suppose that would be an easy one to come up with," he agreed. "How about your health now? Did you have to have the surgery once Hannah was born?"

"Actually the pregnancy helped things. It was like a nine-month reprieve from the damage that was being compounded monthly and there's been an improvement. The doctor says it's likely only a temporary moratorium and I'll still end up having to have the hysterectomy before too long. But for now things are being managed with medication. Which is why Hannah has to be bottle fed. But still, I'm grateful for the improvement, too."

A muted ringing startled Paris. An indication of how tense this conversation was making her.

"I'm sorry, but I need to take this call," Ethan said as he took a tiny cellular phone out of his pants pocket. "There's a situation at the Hong Kong office."

Then he answered the phone with a clipped "Tarlington."

Paris didn't want to appear to be listening in, even though it was impossible not to, so she raised the blanket from over the car seat to look in at Hannah.

The baby was still sleeping soundly, her chubby cheeks like two red rosebuds, one fist pressed to her tiny nub of a nose, her milk-chocolate-colored wisps of hair curled around her head.

The sight of it all made Paris smile.

But for some reason it also caused her to think again about the chat she'd just had with Ethan, and she realized that was the source of her stress.

Had her fibs about when her health problems had been diagnosed and the timetable of Hannah's birth convinced him he had no reason to suspect that he'd been involved in any way in Hannah's conception?

It had seemed like it.

But even so the very fact that he'd asked questions in the first place made her all the more uneasy about having taken this job.

It was too late now, though. So she reminded herself why she'd agreed to it in the first place and that she was going with him to Dunbar to work, not to while away the time with him.

Besides, Paris reasoned, it wasn't as if Hannah had *Tarlington* tattooed across her forehead. There wasn't any reason—beyond the math—for Ethan to think Hannah might be his, and it was Ethan himself who had made the assumption that Paris had gone ahead and had the artificial insemination after their night together.

So maybe it would be all right.

Except that she was going to have to be on guard for the next week.

But that was okay. It was only for a short time, and then she'd have the money for a new car. One short week, in and out, and Ethan Tarlington would never be the wiser.

At least, that was what she was gambling on.

Because no matter how drop-dead gorgeous he was, no matter how many things had been set alive inside her by being with him again and thinking about that night they'd had together, no matter how difficult it had been to keep from thinking about him in the past fourteen months, Paris was not going to let him get too close. To her or to Hannah.

She knew about rich, powerful men, and as Ethan made his demands of whoever he was talking to on the phone at that moment and Paris heard in his voice the unshakable confidence that he could have whatever he wanted and have it his way, she knew she was right.

Rich and powerful men were conquerors. They became accustomed to owning things. And people. To getting what they wanted and to not letting anything stand in the way of that.

And children fit into all of those categories.

Paris knew it from her own experience. From what she'd seen with her own eyes. And she wasn't going to let herself or her baby fall victim to that.

Not under any circumstances.

Not for any man.

Not even for one who looked like Ethan Tarlington and made everything female in her stand up and take notice.

Chapter Three

Ethan's house was on the west side of Dunbar, which meant that they reached it without going through the small town.

There were no signs and not even a mailbox to claim the property as his when the limousine turned off the main road onto a private driveway. The driveway was lined on both sides by red oak trees, the branches reaching out to each other to form an arc overhead that blocked most of the sun's scorching rays.

Paris wasn't sure exactly how far it was to the house, but it had to have been at least a mile before the place even came into view.

And when it did she could hardy believe her eyes.

She'd thought Ethan's house in Denver was impressive. It was three stories of Tudor mansion encompassing twenty-six rooms and an English garden in back.

But the house in Dunbar was even more incredible. It could have been a sprawling, luxury resort.

Granted it was two levels rather than three and it was built of rustic logs. But somehow those rustic logs managed to look refined, and the U-shaped home stretched a full city block around a fountain made to look like a natural rock formation complete with a rippling waterfall.

"Software has been very good to you," she said in awe as the car came to a stop in front of the walkway that led to the oversize, carved double-door entrance.

"I don't have any complaints, that's for sure," he said, again without a drop of swelled-headedness in his attitude.

Ethan leaned to the side to open the door, then straightened up again and motioned with his chiseled chin for Paris to precede him.

"Go ahead and stretch your legs. I'll get the car seat and Hannah," he said.

Paris was quick to decline the offer. "That's okay. I can manage."

But he wasn't having any of that. "I'll be right behind you and I promise not to jiggle her enough to wake her up."

There wasn't much Paris could say to that without sounding rude or making him wonder why she put herself between him and her baby every chance she got. So she had to concede.

"Okay. Thanks," she said as she got out of the car.

It did feel good to stand after the long ride. As good as it was to breathe the fresh, clean, country air perfumed with the scent of wildflowers planted around the rock fountain. And although it had been nice that the interior of the limousine was climate controlled, it was also good to feel the naturally cooling shade of the red oak trees that surrounded the house, too.

"There we go."

Paris heard Ethan's uttering from inside the car and glanced in that direction just as he got out with the baby carrier.

But as Paris reached to take it from him, he said, "Oh-oh. I hear something," and rather than handing over the baby seat, he set it on the roof and looked under the blanket.

At six-four and standing directly in front of the carrier, Ethan had the advantage. When he removed the blanket Paris could see her daughter and that Hannah's big bright aquamarine eyes were open, but she couldn't get to her.

"Yep. Wide-awake. Am I in trouble?" Ethan asked.

"No. She was about due to wake up, anyway." Paris answered with the truth, omitting the fact that she'd been hoping to get Hannah out of sight before it happened, though.

"Can I take her out of this thing?" was Ethan's next question.

"Oh, I don't know about that. You're a stranger and—"

"I don't think she cares. She's smiling at me," he informed Paris. Then, in a softer voice to her daughter, he said, "Hello there, little Hannah. Did you have a nice nap?"

"She's probably wet," Paris said, figuring that could ward off anything.

But not Ethan, who said, "I don't mind."

He didn't wait for any more go-ahead. Instead he unbuckled the carrier's restraints and held out his big hands to the baby.

And what did her ordinarily shy, slightly wary daughter do?

Hannah gave him her biggest grin—the one that put a tiny dimple just over the right side of her mouth—and held her arms out to him, too.

"See, she wants me to hold her," he said as he scooped the baby out of her seat.

He was surprisingly adept at it. He actually set her on his hip like an old pro.

"Can she hold her own head up?" he asked, supporting it until he knew whether or not she needed it.

"Yes, she holds her head up just fine on her own," Paris assured him.

She was itching to snatch Hannah away from him. But she was also struck by how touching—and appealing—was the sight of the big man holding the tiny child so carefully.

"Hi, Hannah," he repeated then. "Remember me?"

Hannah went on grinning at him and, in the process of flailing her arms around in apparent glee, accidentally grabbed his nose.

Ethan laughed. "I think she likes me."

And he seemed to like her.

It was very alarming to Paris.

"I can take her now," she said, reaching for the baby.

"You don't have to. Let me hold her for a minute."

His denial to turn Hannah over when Paris was angling for it raised more red flags in her. Even though she knew it wasn't as if he were actually usurping her child, that was the button it pushed in her.

"Really," she insisted more forcefully. "She has very fair skin and if she's left in a wet diaper for too long she gets a rash."

This time Paris didn't give him the opportunity to refuse her. She took Hannah out of his arms before he could do anything to stop her.

"Maybe we can play later, when your mom's not so nervous," he said to Hannah without seeming to take offense.

Paris doubted that she would spend any of the coming week not being nervous, but she didn't tell him that. Instead, as the limousine driver unloaded suitcases from the trunk, she draped her purse and diaper bag over her shoulder and said, "If you'll point me in the direction of our room I'll just take her inside. Is there a staff wing or something?"

"There's a section of the house where the live-in

staff have rooms of their own, but you and Hannah will be right across the hall from me. I called ahead and made arrangements. My housekeeper should have outfitted Hannah's room with some baby necessities—a crib and whatnot. But you won't be able to find your way without the nickel tour. I was planning to do that this afternoon but now I'll be on the phone to Hong Kong again, so we'll have to save that for tonight after dinner and I'll just have someone else take you to your rooms now.''

''Wait a minute,'' Paris said as she sorted through all the things he'd said. ''We're having dinner together, and you bought furniture, and you're putting us in the room just across the hall from you? I know you said we'd be staying in your house, but you also said it was so big you'd hardly know we were here. There was nothing about having meals together or you buying furniture or my staying across the hall from you.''

''I don't recall saying anything about hardly knowing you'd be here.''

Okay, so maybe that had just been what she'd thought. And planned. But it would be impossible to pull off if she and Hannah were within a few feet of his room the whole time.

''I'm just staff,'' she reminded. ''I shouldn't be staying in a guest room.''

''You're only technically staff. I'm also considering you and Hannah guests.''

''I don't think that's a good idea.''

''Sure it is. I'm looking forward to the pleasure of your company.''

"There's no pleasure in my company," Paris said, too flustered to realize before the words came out how they sounded. But she didn't pause to amend it. Instead she went on to say, "I agreed to this whole arrangement only on a strictly business basis."

"Right. Strictly business. So let's look at it that way. Let's say you were a business consultant who had come to Dunbar at my request to advise me about something. Where would you be staying? Dunbar doesn't have a hotel so you'd be staying here. In the same room you'll be in. Which would make you my guest as well as my business associate. And as my guest, where would you be having your meals? In the kitchen? No. You'd be eating meals with me. And what would you be doing in the evenings or when you had a free afternoon? Would I leave you to twiddle your thumbs? No, I'd be entertaining you. But would it be anything personal? Of course not. It would just be common courtesy and management having its privileges. No big deal."

It was a big deal. This whole thing was turning into a much bigger deal than Paris had anticipated.

But she was beginning to think that it was her own fault for not asking more questions about accommodations and how her nonwork hours might be spent.

"Maybe this wasn't a good idea after all. Maybe Hannah and I should take the next bus back to the city."

"Now why would you want to do that?" Ethan asked, his tone cajoling.

"I meant it when I said what happened between

us before is not going to happen again. I'm here to do a job and that's it. I'm not here to spend a week with you at your country house.''

''Would that be so bad?'' he asked quietly.

It would probably be too good.

''Other people doing jobs around here aren't in guest rooms, they haven't had furniture bought especially for them, and they aren't being wined and dined with members of the family.''

He leaned in closer and said in a warm gust of confidentiality, ''But you aren't *other people*. You are my party coordinator, here at my special request.''

There was just no arguing with him.

And then, too, the man could get to her. He really could. Standing there so tall and handsome, so sexy, and so mischievously sweet on top of everything else...

''Come on,'' he coaxed. ''Let's just call it a middle ground and agree that we can mix business with pleasure as long as the pleasure is just good, clean fun. The same kind of good, clean fun I might have with any business associate I brought out here.''

Again, that was a perspective that was hard to dispute. Especially when she thought once more about the money she needed for a new car and the fact that this simple week's worth of work was going to get that for her.

And if there was the tiniest part of her—deep, deep down—that wanted to stay in this beautiful home for a week, that wanted to spend a little time with Ethan? It was a part she didn't want to acknowledge.

Even as it made her waver. "Good, clean fun and no 'hanky-panky,'" she warned.

"Strictly business when business needs to be attended to. Good, clean fun the rest of the time. And no 'hanky-panky,'" he agreed with a crooked smile when he said hanky-panky.

Paris wondered if she could trust him.

She wasn't too sure she could.

But that tiny part of her that wanted to stay suddenly asserted itself with a surprising strength, and she couldn't force herself to go through with catching the bus back to Denver.

Instead she again reminded herself that Hannah did not have *Tarlington* stamped on her to give away her secret, so they should be relatively safe regardless.

And if Paris saw more of Ethan than she'd originally thought she would?

It wasn't as if she couldn't control herself. Just because he was great-looking and charming, just because she'd succumbed to his appeal once, didn't mean she would do it again. Especially not with his brothers and his house staff around as chaperones and deterrents.

But still she didn't concede gracefully. "Why do I feel as if I was brought here under false pretenses?"

Ethan seemed to know that he'd won because he smiled a wickedly victorious smile and said, "I can't imagine."

His eyes held hers for a moment then. Warm blue eyes that set off something much too titillating in the pit of her stomach and made her wonder if she was doing the right thing.

But the matter seemed to have been resolved and forgotten about when a plump older woman with extremely short gray hair, very red cheeks and a nose with a bulb on the end came out of the house, and Ethan spun toward her to hug her as if he were greeting his mother or his favorite aunt.

"Lolly, Lolly, Lolly, you're looking younger and more beautiful every day," he exclaimed.

"You better believe it," she countered as Paris looked on.

They both had a laugh at that as their hug ended and Ethan turned back to Paris.

"Paris, this is Lolly McGinty. She runs things around here. Lolly, this is Paris Hanley and Hannah."

Paris held out her hand. "It's nice to meet you."

"Likewise."

"Paris is all yours for the afternoon, Lolly," Ethan said when the amenities were concluded. Then, to Paris again, he added, "Lolly will get you set up and fill you in on what's going on with the party while I reconnect with the Hong Kong office and try to sort things out there. Then I'll see you again at dinner."

In other words, she was dismissed. Like any other employee might have been.

And for some reason that chafed a bit.

But she refused to fuel the feeling and instead focused on the housekeeper.

"Lead the way," she said, turning her back on Ethan without another word.

She could feel his gaze on her as she followed Lolly into the house, though.

She did her best to ignore it. To ignore it and the swell of satisfaction she felt at the thought that he might be admiring what he saw.

It was more important to remember that she'd ventured onto thin ice by coming here with him in the first place.

And that anyone on thin ice should tread very carefully.

"So, big A, is it just me or do you feel like old Ethan here has brought us into his den to make some kind of announcement?"

"Could be, Dev, I hear he all of a sudden brought a woman along this year. Could be it has something to do with her."

Ethan let his brothers play their game while he poured the three glasses of twenty-year-old Scotch that was their kickoff to this week in Dunbar.

When he turned from the bar to bring the drinks with him to the high-backed leather chairs where they sat, he said, "Don't take that act out on the road or you'll starve trying to make a living with it."

His brothers just smiled.

"What's the big thing you wanted to talk to us about that couldn't wait until we unpacked and had dinner?" Aiden asked as he accepted his Scotch and sampled it.

"I need your opinion on something."

"Okay, shoot," Devon ordered, savoring a sip from his glass, too.

"The week before I left the country last year I met this woman," Ethan began.

"The woman you brought with you here?"

"Right. Paris Hanley. Anyway, we spent the night together—"

"And you wanted to make sure we knew that you aren't all work and no play?" Aiden goaded.

"Will you cut the jokes? This is serious."

Ethan went on to explain what had led to his discovery that Paris had a baby.

"And you think she's yours?" Devon said when his brother had finished.

"That's the thing—I don't know. Paris claims she had artificial insemination right after our night together and that Hannah was born early. But that could just be a story she's feeding me."

"Oh, I doubt that," Aiden said as if he thought it was far-fetched.

"You can't say Hannah isn't mine until you see her," Ethan insisted. "Until you see if you see the same thing in her that I do." Although, Ethan hadn't told his brothers what it was he thought he recognized in Hannah because he didn't want to influence them.

"Look around you, Ethan," Aiden said, continuing to support his position. "You're a big-bucks guy. If this woman—or any woman—ended up having your baby, she would want child support from you. She'd be crazy not to come after you with both barrels."

"That's what makes the whole thing so damn weird. But I'm telling you, I think Hannah is mine."

"But you didn't ask point-blank," Devon said.

"No, I didn't and I don't want to. Not until I know I'm not imagining what I see in Hannah. And if you guys see what I see and I'm *not* imagining it, then I still don't want to ask outright until I get some sort of handle on what possible reason Paris could have for keeping the truth from me."

"It's not really ethical but I could do a blood test on the baby behind Mom's back," Aiden offered. "It wouldn't be as conclusive as testing you both for a DNA match but it would be a start. Maybe rule you out from the get-go."

Ethan shook his head. "I couldn't do that. It's too sneaky and deceitful."

"And what do you call it if the baby is yours and the mother is pretending she isn't?" Devon asked.

"I call it sneaky and deceitful. And something I want to know, if that's what Paris is."

"Ah," Aiden muttered, setting his half-empty glass on the end table. "So what we have here is also a test for the mom. To see if she's like Bettina."

"Which means you must like Paris—a minor detail you left out," Devon concluded.

"I just want to know the truth," Ethan said. "And why she isn't telling me I'm Hannah's father if I *am* Hannah's father."

"Do you *want* the baby to be yours?" Aiden asked then.

"I don't know," he answered honestly. "The whole thing has blindsided me. I guess for the moment I just want you two to take a close look at Hannah and tell me what you think."

"And if what we think is that she's yours?" Devon asked.

Ethan took the last drink of his Scotch and then stared into the empty glass. "I don't know the answer to that, either. I'm just flyin' by the seat of my pants on this."

And wishing along the way that he could stop noticing that Paris had a laugh like wind chimes and eyes that sparkled like stars and lips so pink and soft they put rose petals to shame....

Paris spent the afternoon with Lolly. The older woman brought her up to speed on all the party preparations and helped her and Hannah settle in.

They finished just as Hannah was ready for her dinner, and by the time Paris had fed her daughter and put her down for the night, Paris was smeared with strained pears and needed to change for her own dinner.

Her clothes were all hung in an opulent walk-in closet, so that was where she went in search of something to wear, trying not to think about Ethan as she did.

Why should it matter what he might like or what might make her waist look smallest or her rear end look firmest or her breasts look a little larger than they were?

It shouldn't.

But as she stood surveying her choices, she suddenly regretted that her limited budget had left her wardrobe on the practical side. And since she'd expected this to be a working trip, she'd only brought the most practical, at that.

Well, since she'd expected this to be a working trip and because she'd steadfastly held to the determination that she would not be fraternizing with Ethan, she had no need to be overly concerned with what she looked like.

Except, now that she actually was going to fraternize with him, she *did* care.

Luckily Lolly had said casual attire was the norm, so even though Paris didn't have anything she considered impressive, she wouldn't be underdressed.

She assumed jeans were too casual, though, and opted for a pair of gray twill slacks and a plain white blouse with a banded collar.

The closet was actually more like a dressing room, allowing her to change right there before going back into the bedroom to freshen her mascara and blush and put a comb through her hair.

As she did she couldn't help marveling yet again at the room itself and the bathroom connected to it.

The bathroom was a study in luxury, with a navy-blue marble floor, countertops, shower stall and wainscoting halfway up the walls. It also had a sunken tub with a whirlpool she could switch on at the touch of a button, and an octagonal stained-glass window on the wall behind it.

The bedroom had a king-size brass bed with an ornate scroll design in the headboard and the footboard, as well as four tall posts that reached up to hold a fringed canopy. The mattress was covered in a hand-stitched country quilt and stacked with half a dozen fluffy pillows covered in shams that matched different patterns in the quilt.

There were two bureaus—one tall and strictly for clothing and linens, the other long and low. The lower of the two contained a fully stocked bar in one section and an equally well-equipped refrigerated drawer in another. Plus the push of a button here, too, raised the top of the bureau and out came a complete entertainment center.

In addition to the bureaus, there was an armoire and the matching dressing table Paris was using at that moment, plus a fainting couch and two overstuffed chairs positioned around a fireplace with a carved mantel. And still there was enough floor space left over for aerobic exercise or ballroom dancing.

And this was only a guest room. She couldn't imagine what the master suite was like.

Although that was something she *shouldn't* be imagining, she reminded herself. Ethan's bedroom was so off-limits it shouldn't even be a passing thought.

Yet there she was, wondering about it, anyway. And worse than that, picturing Ethan in it. With maybe just a towel around his waist, his chest and shoulders bare and muscular, his stomach flat, and that line of hair from his navel downward...

''Oh, that's not good,'' she informed herself, closing her eyes as if that would block the mental picture.

Then she opened them again and forced her focus onto herself to make sure she was at least presentable.

Presentable. As in: he was caviar and she was

mashed potatoes. And that was something she had to remember. Despite the fact that she secretly wished she was so stunning it would take his breath away.

Which was also something she shouldn't be thinking, let alone wishing for.

"Strictly business," she told her reflection, much more sternly than she'd ever said it to Ethan.

Then she turned away from the mirror and moved on silent steps across carpeting that was so thick it was almost like walking through unmowed lawn.

Wanting to check on Hannah before she left for dinner, Paris went through the connecting door into Hannah's room.

Hannah's room was every bit as incredible as Paris's. The regular bed had been removed to accommodate an array of Jenny Lind furniture—crib, dresser, changing table, playpen and a matching rocking chair that was not only beautiful but more comfortable than the one Paris had at home.

It was all slightly mind-boggling. Especially to someone who clipped coupons not only for groceries but for haircuts, too.

Hannah was sleeping soundly, and since the air-conditioned room was slightly cool, Paris pulled the blanket over her and allowed herself a few minutes of unbridled joy at the sight.

There had never been anything or anyone Paris loved the way she loved Hannah.

And that, coupled with the splendor of their accommodations, only reinforced her determination to keep her secret about Hannah.

She had seen what the wealth and power of a

prominent surgeon could do to a woman of lesser means. She'd seen how ruthless that wealth and power could make a man and how helpless those lesser means could leave a woman. And Jason's wealth and power had obviously been nothing compared to Ethan's.

It was definitely better that Ethan not know Hannah was his daughter.

Paris bent over the crib railing and kissed the baby's head, wishing just a kiss could somehow brand Hannah as hers and chase away the feeling that something—or someone—could take her baby away from her.

Then she took the portable portion of a state-of-the-art baby monitor from Hannah's dresser, clipped it to her belt and left the room.

Paris hadn't seen much of the rest of the house yet, but Lolly had told her she need only retrace her path to the front entrance where Ethan and his brothers would be through the doors to the left waiting for her in the den.

Paris thought retracing her steps might be easier said than done but she didn't do too badly in finding her way.

When she reached the foyer she checked the baby monitor to make sure she could hear Hannah, smiling at the sucking noise her daughter sometimes made in her sleep and feeling reassured that she would be alerted if the baby woke up. Then she turned to the den's doors and knocked a split second before it opened.

"There you are! I was just going to see if you

were lost,'' Ethan said from the opposite side of the doorway.

''I was feeding Hannah and getting her to sleep. You didn't need to wait for me.''

Ethan grinned. ''Yes, I did.'' Then he gave her the once-over and added, ''Besides, it was worth the wait.''

The compliment and the appreciative, slightly insinuative smile that went with it thrilled Paris more than she wanted to admit. But how could it not when she was a mere five months away from maternity tops and elastic panels in her pants, and there he was, tall and handsome and making every fiber of her being stand up and take notice?

He hadn't changed clothes. He was still wearing the khaki slacks and garnet-colored polo shirt he'd had on when he'd picked her up that morning. But they didn't look any the worse for wear. And neither did he.

He was freshly shaved, and the scent of a woodsy cologne wafted out to her.

She tried not to think about how much she liked it. Or how much she liked that first glimpse of him after not having seen him since that morning.

But it was all there, anyway, just below the surface as he stepped back and said, ''Come on in and meet my brothers. They got in about an hour ago.''

Paris went into the room, taking one long whiff of him as she passed by but promising herself that would be her only indulgence.

The den was paneled in dark oak, furnished in

tufted leather and antique wood and lit by library lamps so it was very cozy and restful.

The other two men stood when she entered the room, and Paris's first thought was that the Tarlingtons were a big lot. When they got to their feet, both of Ethan's brothers rose to more than six feet. And they were as handsome as they were tall and well built.

"Hello," she greeted.

They returned her hello as Ethan came up beside her to perform the introductions.

"This is Aiden, in from Alaska. He's a doctor up there, family medicine. And this is Devon, our wildman wildlife photographer. He globe-trots but calls Denver home base."

Aiden had lighter-blue eyes than Ethan or Devon, and Devon had sort of a bad-boy air about him, but the three of them together looked so much alike that no one would ever doubt they were brothers.

"And this is Paris," Ethan concluded, "who is probably as starved as we are, so shall we go in to eat?"

There was general agreement and then the three men escorted her out of the den, down the hallway and to a dining room that Ethan referred to as the small dining room.

It was larger than the kitchen, dining room and living room combined in Paris's house, but she had the impression that it was probably the everyday dining room because it was more warm and homey than fancy, with a sideboard taking up one wall, a curio cabinet on another and an oblong walnut table in the center.

Ethan seated her at the place setting at the head of the table as if she were the guest of honor and only then did he and his brothers sit down.

"Paris the party planner, huh?" Devon said as the first course—lobster parfait—was served.

"I'm not ordinarily a party planner, no," Paris answered. "It's just that I've avoided taking a nine-to-five job since I graduated from art school so that I can paint."

That seemed to spark Devon's curiosity particularly. "Have you had any gallery showings?"

"A few."

"Successful?"

"Enough so that I'm slowly gaining a following. But I'm still not earning enough from the sale of my work to make a comfortable living. So, to supplement my income, I take whatever temporary job I can that doesn't interfere too much with my artwork or with the time I spend with my daughter."

That led to questions about what kind of odd jobs she might have had and the conversation flowed from there as Paris found Ethan's brothers to be as easy to talk to as he was, and as intelligent and funny and charming, too.

But as the meal progressed, even though she was enjoying herself, Paris also began to be aware of something in her that she didn't want to be aware of.

She was itching to be alone with Ethan.

She knew it would be a mistake. She knew it was

unwise. She knew she shouldn't even allow it if something were to happen and they were left alone.

But more than itching for it, she actually began to will his brothers to excuse themselves. In fact, that was so much on her mind that, at one point, she lost track of the conversation and had to admit her mind had wandered.

And then, just as she was mentally taking herself to task for it, Ethan himself turned to her and said, "How about that tour of the house now? I'm sure these guys will survive if we duck out on them."

His brothers encouraged them to go and all thoughts of not allowing herself to be alone with Ethan fled from her mind like horses from a lightning strike.

She told herself she was only doing it so she could get her bearings in the house. That it was pure necessity.

But the fact that something inside her took wing the moment they left the table made a lie out of it.

There were more than twenty rooms in the house and, as Ethan explained the basic floor plan, all Paris could think was, Good, then it will be a long tour.

But even though her every sense seemed filled by his presence along the way, she still found herself in awe of his home.

Each room was larger and more amazing than the next. Restaurant-size kitchen. Formal dining room. Breakfast room. Den. Formal living room. Family room. Ethan's office. A library. A movie theater. A bowling alley. A full basketball court. And that was only on the first floor.

Upstairs there were eight bedrooms—all of them with private bathrooms. There were also two sitting rooms and a sound-proof music room where, Ethan confided, both he and his brothers had been known to blast their music and play a little air guitar when no one was supposed to be looking.

"And that's it," he said as they reached the door to Paris's room an hour later.

Well, that wasn't *completely* it since he hadn't shown her his rooms across the hall, but it seemed obvious that he didn't intend to, and she knew that was for the best, so she didn't point it out.

"Think you'll be able to find your way around all right?" he asked then.

"I think so. The layout isn't too complicated."

"And there are intercoms in all the rooms so if you get stuck you can just call for help."

"I'm sure I'll be fine."

And that really did seem to be that—the natural conclusion to the evening.

Paris waited for him to say good-night, knowing it was for the best and yet feeling her own spirits sink slightly.

But Ethan didn't say good-night. He leaned one shoulder against the wall next to her door, crossed his arms over his chest, one ankle over the other and said, "So how did this afternoon go? Did Lolly tell you all you needed to know?"

"She told me enough to make it clear that there isn't much for me to do for your party. I'll make a few phone calls to suppliers who are late with deliveries and inventory things as they come in, but for the most part everything is under control.''

"I told you it was. But those phone calls and inventories are things I'd have to do and now I won't. That's worth a lot to me.''

She thought it was worth a lot more to her but she didn't say that.

"How about if tomorrow I show you around Dunbar?'' Ethan said then. "You should have the lay of the land, and I'll introduce you to the people you'll be dealing with when they bring things in for the party or come in to set up or serve or cook. We'll make a day of it.''

Together. Just what she knew she should be avoiding. But they'd already had the discussion about her spending nonwork time with him, and Paris had lost that battle. She knew it was useless to argue about spending work time with him.

And if the prospect had suddenly raised her deflated spirits again? She didn't want to consider why that was.

"Will Lolly watch Hannah, do you think?''

"I'm sure she will. Or we could take Hannah along if you'd rather. I don't mind.''

"That's not a good idea. She needs naps and feedings, and I don't like her to be out in the sun too long.''

"Okay, then we'll have Lolly baby-sit.''

With that settled, Paris again expected him to say good-night.

But again he didn't. He just stayed leaning against the wall, studying her.

"I'm really glad you're here," he said then, as if it were a confession. "I've thought about you a lot since the night we met."

She definitely didn't want to talk about that night. Or how much she'd thought about him since then, too.

Especially not when the air around them seemed to have already taken a shift to intimacy.

So instead she said, "I should probably go in and check on Hannah."

But Ethan ignored the exit line and just went on looking into her eyes. "It's almost like I've been carrying around a part of you since then."

And certainly she'd been carrying around a part of—him...

But again, not something she wanted to say. Any more than she wanted to feel the warm rush his words were sending through her.

"Things are different now," she reminded him. "I'm working for you."

His smile was crooked and devilish. "You're working for me, all right."

In spite of herself, Paris smiled at his innuendo-laced turn of the phrase.

Then in a quiet voice she said, "Don't do this to me, okay?"

"Don't do what to you? I'm just standing here, enjoying the view."

"That—don't flirt and compliment me and be nice and—"

Did he have to have eyes so blue they made it hard for her to maintain her train of thought? Did he have to look at her that way? Did he have to smile that secret smile that seemed to say he hadn't forgotten a single thing about that night they'd shared?

"What do you want me to do? Insult you?" he asked.

It would make things a lot easier on her.

"You know what I want." At least what she'd *told* him she wanted. But every minute that he stood there made her want something entirely different.

Still she said, "I want a business relationship and that's all."

"Are you sure that's all?" he asked in a soft, husky voice.

And as he did, he leaned forward. Just slightly.

Was he testing her resolve? Wondering what she would do?

Or was he actually going to kiss her?

"Yes, I'm sure," Paris said before she'd decided which it was.

But her own tone was almost a whisper because her resolve really was weak. So weak that at that same moment her chin tilted upward just a bit all on its own and her gaze attached itself to his lips. Sensual lips that she'd once felt all over her body. That, deep down, she was screaming to feel again....

But just as she thought he really was going to close the last of that distance between them and press his mouth to hers, he took her at her word and drew back.

"Maybe you're right," he said.

There was actually a part of Paris that told her to say, *No, never mind, I wasn't right. I was so not right*. A part of her that craved that almost-kiss so much that there wasn't a single thing more important than that.

But of course there was.

So Paris drew back, too, standing a little taller, a little straighter, a little stronger than she felt.

And now it seemed as if the ball was in her court.

So, in a stronger voice which concealed the fact that she still felt like mush inside, she said, "I'll see you tomorrow."

"Sleep well," he answered.

Paris raised her chin again, this time only in acknowledgment, and slipped into her room, closing the door behind her.

But quite a few minutes passed before she heard Ethan push off the wall outside her door. Before she heard the door across the hall open and close. Before she moved from just inside hers.

And as she did she wondered if it was possible that she was even more attracted to him now than she had been fourteen months ago.

Because that was almost how it seemed.

Of course, it didn't help matters that he was simply the sexiest man she'd ever encountered. Or that something about him drew her to him.

Not that it made any difference, though. Because she wasn't going to act on it.

But the way things were shaping up, it was going to be a long week.

A very long week.

A very long and uncomfortable week if she didn't nip in the bud things like wanting him to kiss her.

Wanting him to kiss her so badly that it was still a living, breathing thing inside her.

But it wasn't going to happen. She swore to herself that it wasn't.

She had too much at stake.

But she also knew that it was no wonder she'd succumbed to Ethan that night fourteen months ago.

Because falling into his arms, giving herself over to him with wanton abandon, was a fierce urge that was running through her all over again.

Chapter Four

Although Ethan spent as much time in Dunbar as he could, the week of his annual party was usually the only week out of the year that he planned on total rest and relaxation. But that still didn't mean he could make himself sleep late in the mornings, and so, even without an alarm clock, he was awake to watch the sun rise the next day.

He wasn't thinking about the beauty of it, though. His mind was wandering. Just the way it had been wandering so much since Friday. So much since he'd met Paris, really. But more since Friday.

He felt as if he should be angry with her. He knew he should be leery of her. Certainly he should be totally turned off by her and the idea that she could be hiding something as monumental as the fact that Hannah might be his child.

But he wasn't any of those things. He couldn't even make himself be when he tried.

And he *did* try. He told himself over and over again that Paris could be lying to him. Lying to him on a bigger scale than Bettina ever had.

But it didn't work.

Yes, he knew intellectually that he should be barely able to tolerate someone who could even potentially be doing such a thing.

But on an emotional level?

That was a different story altogether.

There was just something about her.

Something more than a great body. More than silken hair and luminous skin. More than shining silver eyes. Something more, even, than the pure, raw sexual attraction to her that made him want to feel her compact body against him, that made him want to wrap his arms around her, kiss her, touch her, do more than just kiss her and touch her.

There was also something about her that reached out and drew him in. Something about her that, whenever she walked into a room, caused everything else to pale and fade into the background for him.

He was intrigued by Paris Hanley, and there was nothing he could do about it. As intrigued as he'd been the night they'd met. Maybe more intrigued.

Actually, maybe the whole baby thing was adding to her intrigue, he thought. Because he still hadn't come up with any idea why she would keep it from him if it were true, and the mystery of that was an intrigue all its own.

And if Hannah *was* his child, Paris was most definitely keeping it a mystery.

But for the life of him he couldn't understand why.

He just didn't have an answer for it, and it was driving him crazy.

Unless the answer was the only obvious one and Hannah really *wasn't* his.

He hadn't thought as much about that as he'd thought about her being his baby.

But now he considered it more seriously.

What if he was just imagining what he thought he saw in Hannah? What if it was some kind of trick his brain was playing on him? Or just a coincidence?

Was that possible?

Anything was possible.

And what if Hannah really wasn't his? he asked himself. What if Paris really had had artificial insemination and wasn't keeping anything from him after all? What then?

Free sailing.

That was the first thing that came into Ethan's head. He could have free sailing with Paris because it would mean she wasn't like Bettina. That Paris was on the up and up.

And maybe that was the truth and that was why, deep down, he couldn't be angry with her or leery of her or turned off by her.

It made a certain amount of sense to him.

It made more sense, he reasoned, than that Hannah was his and Paris was keeping it a secret from him rather than asking him for the help she so obviously needed.

It made a whole lot more sense. And it was definitely a scenario he liked better, so he worked to embrace it.

Because if Paris was being honest with him, then this week didn't have to have a cloud hanging over it. And he could genuinely relax and let go and enjoy himself. Enjoy Paris.

Oh, yeah, he liked that scenario a whole lot better.

So why not? Why not give her the benefit of the doubt? She wasn't Bettina, and as far as he knew for sure, Paris hadn't earned his distrust.

So figure that you're wrong and Paris isn't hiding anything.

Or at least give it a try.

He could do that, couldn't he?

He thought he could. He knew he wanted to.

So, with a renewed eagerness to face the day—a day he was spending with Paris—Ethan pushed off the French doors he'd been leaning against to watch the sunrise and decided he needed a cup of coffee.

He grabbed his robe from the foot of his bed and put it on, cinching it around his waist before he left his rooms, even though he was relatively sure he was the only one in the house who was up yet.

But he got just a few feet out the door when he heard something that told him he *wasn't* the only early riser.

Something high-pitched and lilting and sweet.

It was coming from Hannah's room.

He moved closer to her door and nearly pressed his ear to the panel to listen.

Cooing. The baby was cooing.

It made him smile.

It also made him want to see her.

So he ventured a light tap on the door with just one knuckle.

There was no response from inside. All he heard were more baby sounds.

It occurred to him then that Paris might not be up yet. That maybe only Hannah was awake.

He knocked again, but when there still wasn't any response he eased the door open and stuck his head inside.

Paris was nowhere in sight and so Ethan went into the room.

Early daylight came through the curtains to lend a rosy glow as he crossed to the crib.

Hannah was wide-awake, lying on her back, holding one foot in each hand.

She turned her head to him when he came up to the side of the crib and instantly gave him a huge grin.

"Good morning, little lady," he whispered to her.

She gurgled at him as if in answer and that made him laugh quietly.

"Whatcha got there?" he asked, rubbing the very tips of her chubby toes with a single index finger.

Hannah let go of her feet and grabbed his finger with one of her free hands, cooing this time the way he'd heard her from out in the hall.

Ethan wiggled his finger for her, delighting her. And him, too.

And in that moment all the reasoning he'd just done, all the benefit of the doubt he'd thought to give

Paris, flew out the window. Because he saw all over again in Hannah what he'd seen on Friday.

He saw his mother.

He saw her in Hannah's aquamarine eyes. And he also saw something he hadn't seen before—he saw a dimple that appeared over the corner of the baby's mouth when she smiled. The same dimple that his mother had had in the same spot.

And he knew he wasn't imagining it—not what he was seeing and not what he was feeling, either. Because as he stood there with Hannah's tiny hand clinging to his finger, something welled up in his chest and told him she was his.

No, it wasn't conclusive proof. Not the eyes. Not the dimple. Not the swell of his heart. But he believed Hannah was his, anyway.

And that put him right back to square one—if she was his, why didn't Paris admit it?

It was enough to drive him crazy.

So maybe he should just force the issue, he thought. Maybe he should confront her. Demand to know the truth. Maybe insist on DNA testing to give himself some peace.

But a split second after considering that he knew he wasn't going to do any of it. It was a hard line he just wasn't ready to take. Not yet, anyway.

Yes, he hated thinking that Hannah might be his child and Paris wasn't telling him. He hated thinking Paris was lying to him.

But he hated more the mental picture he got when he thought about calling her on it. He hated more the picture of the two of them on opposite sides.

So maybe if he couldn't give her the benefit of the doubt about Hannah, he could at least try to keep an open mind about *why* Paris wasn't telling him the truth. He could trust that she had a good reason and that if he gave her some time, if he let her know she could trust him, she might let him know what was going on in that pretty head of hers.

Because after fourteen months of thinking about her, of wanting to see her again, after finally getting her here where he could be with her every day, he couldn't make himself give that up. And even if it was only for a week, it was still a week he wouldn't have if he forced the issue of what he believed about Hannah.

The baby let go of his finger then and made a sound that almost seemed like a giggle as she kicked her legs up in the air and grabbed her toes once more.

And that was another thing, Ethan thought. He wanted a little time with Hannah, too. A little time to sort out how he felt about the possibility of fatherhood.

The door that connected Hannah's room to Paris's opened and there was Paris.

Ethan saw the surprise in her face just before she jumped behind the door so he wouldn't see her in the big Tweety Bird T-shirt she apparently wore as pajamas.

"I was just going to the kitchen for coffee and I heard Hannah in here," Ethan explained from the distance. "I thought I'd look in on her."

"I'll take care of her," Paris called back, still out of sight.

Ethan glanced at the baby again, rubbing the top of her head with only two fingertips. "She's pretty cute in the morning."

"I better get her changed and fed or she won't be for long."

Ethan got the hint. "Okay, I'm going."

But he didn't go immediately. He allowed himself one more look at Hannah, at his mother in Hannah, before he finally retraced his steps to the hall door.

"The coast is clear. See you later," he called to Paris, and then he closed the door behind him.

But as he paused in the hallway, picturing Paris with her hair sleep-tousled, padding to the crib in her Tweety Bird T-shirt and picking up her daughter to hold her for the first time that day, he knew for sure that he was going to temporarily let lie whatever was going on with Paris, that he was going to give her the chance to be open and honest with him.

And if Paris still hadn't told him what he believed was the truth by the end of the week, he'd have to push it.

But he hoped it didn't come to that.

And if it didn't, then maybe they could go from there.

Because just that momentary glimpse of her was enough to churn things up inside him. Enough to make that one night they'd spent together an even more vivid memory than it had been.

Just that momentary glimpse of her was enough to make him want to take her hand and lead her back into her room, leaving Hannah to entertain herself a little longer while he entertained Hannah's mom....

* * *

Despite the plans for Ethan to show Paris around Dunbar, most of that day passed without her seeing him again after her morning's surprise.

According to Lolly, his brothers had talked him into a horseback ride, and so the trip to Dunbar was postponed until late in the afternoon.

"That's okay," Paris told the older woman, thinking that maybe keeping her distance from Ethan might be possible after all. "I wanted to get right to work on those delinquent suppliers, anyway. In fact, this is much better."

And she'd meant it, too. It was good to get busy and earn the exorbitant fee Ethan was paying her. It was good to have a calm day with Hannah, especially when they were both in new and unfamiliar surroundings with a lot of strangers around them. It was good that Paris could put Hannah down for her naps and be there when she woke up. It was good that Paris didn't have to be with Ethan.

But did it *feel* good?

It didn't.

In fact, it spoiled Paris's mood altogether. And no matter how hard she tried not to analyze why that was, she still knew that what was running rampant through her was plain old disappointment.

Because as much as she'd told herself otherwise, she'd been looking forward to having all day with Ethan.

It's a warning sign, she told herself.

A warning sign she needed to pay attention to.

She knew she was particularly susceptible to the

man. How could she deny that when she'd already spent the night with him? Being disappointed at not seeing as much of him as she'd thought she was going to was an indication that she was every bit as susceptible to him now as she had been then.

And that was something she had to watch out for. Something she had to fight.

So she went through the day tending to business and her baby and tamping down every thought of Ethan the minute one popped into her head.

But then three o'clock came and Lolly arrived at the door to the den where Paris was going over party preparations, announcing that Ethan was back from his ride and ready to go into Dunbar whenever she was.

And the sun suddenly seemed to shine a little brighter, and nothing Paris did, nothing she told herself, made it dim again.

Just watch yourself, she cautioned.

And she had every intention of doing just that.

Even as she changed out of the looser-fitting pants and top she had on and replaced them with a pair of pencil-thin black spandex capri slacks and a body-hugging funnel-neck sleeveless T-shirt.

Both of which were a long way from her very unsexy Tweety Bird nightshirt.

But the clothes notwithstanding, she swore she wasn't going to give in to her weakness for Ethan Tarlington.

She would merely accept his tour of the town and maintain an attitude of professionalism the whole time…. If it was the last thing she ever did.

And if her tighter outfit made him regret keeping her waiting for him?

It served him right.

Dunbar was hardly the sleepy small town Paris had expected. It wasn't a bustling metropolis, either, but it was a medium-size community with a half-dozen streets lined with shops—and businesses at its heart and a widespread residential area sprouting out in all directions around it.

The first thing that struck Paris about it was how clean and well kept everything was. Granted, she was viewing it from a distance as Ethan drove the SUV that had replaced the limousine that had brought them from Denver, but still she didn't see a single spot of peeling paint or a missing shutter or even a lopsided sign on the mostly post-World War II era buildings.

There were some newer structures, too, that had crept in among the mom-and-pop diner and the old-fashioned, counter-service ice-cream parlor and the family-owned-and-operated hardware store. Two rivaling grocery chains had built markets that had a more contemporary look to them, the major fast-food establishments had set up shop in their own distinctive styles, and there was the requisite Starbucks, as well as a gas station complete with minimart.

But for the most part it seemed as if the best use was made of the spaces already available from years gone by so that the small-town flavor hadn't been lost.

And that small-town flavor was particularly evident when Ethan parked the car so they could walk.

It seemed as if nearly every person they passed on the street either greeted Ethan by name or stopped to talk to him as if he were the prodigal son returning home.

After a while Paris began to wonder about it. But with so many people wanting to say hello to Ethan, there wasn't an opportunity to ask why he was so popular.

It was nearly six before Paris had met the retailers and service providers she would be working with, and by then it was too late for Ethan to finish the tour with the headquarters of Tarlington Software.

He did drive her past it, though.

It was an enormous, old, red stone factory that had been renovated with an eye toward retaining the original design.

Paris was curious about the fact that Dunbar Steel Foundry was carved into a granite arch above the main entrance, but just as she was on the verge of asking about it, Ethan had to answer his cell phone.

They were all the way back home again before that call ended and by then he'd moved on to a different topic.

"I asked Lolly if we could eat earlier tonight so Hannah could join us," he informed Paris once he'd rounded the SUV and opened her door for her. "Is that okay?"

"She's not much of a conversationalist. I don't know why you'd want her to have dinner with everyone."

"I just thought it would be fun. And nicer for you than hiding away somewhere with her. Let's do it this once and see how it goes. And if you'd rather go back to the way it was last night after this, we will."

So again he was making sure he got his way. Just as Jason always had.

Paris bristled slightly at that.

Of course, by then she was bristling slightly over the fact that he hadn't shown any signs of noticing her tighter clothes—or being affected by them—so she might have been nitpicking a little. Especially since *she* had noticed right off the bat that he'd shaved and showered after his horseback ride and that he looked fresh and smelled wonderful. And that seeing him in blue jeans and the navy T-shirt that managed to be casual and yet dressy, too, was a treat worth waiting for because no jeans and T-shirt had ever fit anyone as well. Or as sexily.

But under the circumstances what could she say?

"I guess it'll be all right if I feed Hannah in the dining room while everyone else eats. For tonight. But I really don't think you want to make a habit of it."

"We'll see you both in a little bit, then," Ethan said as they went into the house.

"Okay, but expect an I-told-you-so if you end up with baby food all over that nice carpeting in the dining room. Out of the blue she can spit it everywhere."

That idea seemed to amuse him. "Shall I wear a raincoat?"

"Just be prepared."

But Paris didn't end up getting to say "I told you so" because Hannah couldn't have been a better dinner companion.

With the infant seat strapped into the high chair, Hannah could see all three Tarlington men and it was clearly a view she liked. She smiled for them. She cooed for them. She waved her arms and kicked her legs in delight for them. And she ate without so much as dribbling a drop down her chin.

For their part, Ethan and his brothers seemed to enjoy Hannah just as much. They showed a surprising interest in her and in what she could and couldn't do, in what her routine was and how many hours of sleep she needed and how she made her wants and needs known.

It occurred to Paris that they might just be being polite but if that was the case they hid it well because by the time the meal was over and Hannah's bedtime had arrived, they all seemed as sorry to lose her as kids having their new toy put away.

Although Ethan didn't merely accept that. He asked if he could tag along and watch Paris put Hannah to bed.

"There isn't a whole lot to it," Paris told him. "I change her diaper, put on her pajamas, give her a bottle, and she's usually out like a light by the time I put her in her crib."

But he insisted he wanted to watch, and so that was what he did.

It was only when it was all done and Hannah was tucked in that Paris wondered if maybe Ethan had

had an ulterior motive. Because that was when he said, "Let's go into the den and have a nightcap—I have a new bottle of cream sherry from Napa Valley that's so smooth you hardly know it's going down. I think you'll like it."

He was pretty smooth himself with the way he'd slipped that in as if it were a given that they would be spending the rest of the evening together, she thought.

Still, smooth or not, she knew she should say thanks, but no thanks.

Except that what she knew and what she was inclined toward were two different things.

After all, it *was* only eight o'clock. And her sole other option was watching television in her room.

Hmm. Close the day with a glass of sherry and the company of a man who could fill out a pair of jeans like nobody's business? Or sit alone in her room and watch reruns?

The scales were tipped heavily in his favor.

Heavily enough to outweigh her better judgment.

It was only a harmless nightcap, she reasoned. It didn't have to mean anything and it didn't have to go any further than that.

"Maybe just a quick one," she finally agreed.

Then she grabbed the baby monitor and followed Ethan.

And if following him caused her eyes to stray to his backside? If it left her admiring the way the denim rode his tight buns?

It was purely accidental.

But it also made her stomach flutter in a way that it shouldn't have.

"Maybe your brothers would like to try the sherry, too," Paris said when they reached the den, thinking that there was safety in numbers.

"Are you nervous about being alone with me?" he asked as he went to the bar built into the paneling of one wall.

"I wouldn't say I was nervous, no. Why would I be nervous?" she said nervously.

"I don't know, why would you be?"

"I wouldn't be. I'm not."

"Then we don't need my brothers."

Ethan turned from the bar with a glass of sherry in each hand and motioned with one of them to the section of the room where a leather sofa and two matching chairs were positioned around a low coffee table.

It took Paris a moment for the meaning of that motion to sink in, though, because her gaze had gone to his hands and she got lost in an instant flash of what it had felt like to have those same big, strong, adept hands on her body.

Then she yanked herself out of that memory and the unwanted tingling her flesh had answered it with and went to one of the chairs.

Ethan handed her a sherry when she was seated and then took the chair across from her. All the way across the very large, square box coffee table.

She'd purposely avoided the couch so there was no chance of their sitting close together there. But still, the fact that he added to the distance rather than taking a spot on the sofa to at least be slightly nearer to her raised the same disappointment she'd felt when he'd postponed their trip into Dunbar today.

It was crazy and she knew it. But there it was.

She reminded herself that she really did want to keep things on an impersonal basis with him. And sitting far apart definitely accomplished that.

Yet there was also a small, totally illogical part of her that would have liked him to pursue her anyway. The way he had the night they'd met. Even in the face of her rejection of him.

But that part of her that would have liked to be pursued no matter what was probably just ego, she told herself. And it didn't need to be paid attention to.

So she tried not to.

Instead she attempted to distract herself by finally asking the question she would have asked on the way home had he not been on the cell phone.

"Why does it say Dunbar Steel Foundry over the entrance to Tarlington Software?"

"Because that's what it was for nearly a hundred years before. Dunbar was the name of the town's founding family. They built the town around the steel foundry and until about ten years ago that's what kept almost everybody here going, in one way or another."

"What happened ten years ago?"

"The last of the Dunbars died off and the foundation that inherited everything closed down the foundry without a thought about what it would do to the whole economy of Dunbar."

"And you stepped in?"

"It was the least I could do. I bought the foundry, remodeled it to meet the needs of manufacturing and distributing our line of mass-market software and games, and then retrained everybody so they could do that instead of steelwork."

"You turned steelworkers into computer geeks?"

"Don't sound so amazed. It wasn't that hard for a lot of people, and the ones who couldn't grasp the technical stuff were put in other areas they *could* handle. It worked out all the way around, if I do say so myself."

No wonder he was so popular. He was the town's savior.

"You said it was the least you could do—what does that mean?"

He didn't answer that right away. He pointed toward her glass with the chin she suddenly remembered kissing in the process of kissing her way from the hollow below one of his ears, along his jaw to the hollow of the other...

"How's the sherry?" he asked.

"Good," she said with a quiet catch in her voice.

But, quiet or not, he heard it anyway.

"If you don't like it I can get you something else."

She took a sip to prove she did like it. And also in hopes that the fiery alcohol would cauterize her unruly thoughts.

Then she said, "No, I really do like it," in a more controlled tone.

Apparently satisfied, Ethan finally answered her question.

"Bringing Tarlington Software here was the least I could do because this town raised my brothers and me."

"The whole town?"

"A big part of it. The population was considerably less then—a lot of people have moved in since I brought the software business here. But still there was a joining of forces to keep Aiden, Devon and me in Dunbar after our parents were killed in a car accident just outside of town."

"When was this?"

"I was ten. Aiden was nine. Devon, eight. We didn't have any other family so we were orphaned, and if it hadn't been for the efforts of a whole lot of our neighbors we would have been separated and put in foster care. We'd have probably lost each other."

"And the town didn't let that happen?"

Ethan nodded and took a sip of his sherry.

Paris fought not to be so aware of a lot of the little things he did. Like the way he tilted his head back slightly to drink from the sherry glass, letting her see his Adam's apple—another spot she'd taken a turn kissing. Or his mouth on the glass's edge the way it had been on her mouth once upon a time....

Then he said, "No, the town didn't let anything happen to separate us. But the foundry didn't pay all that well, so folks around here were just making ends meet. Nobody could afford to take on three growing boys alone. So a fair share of the townsfolk formed a sort of coalition to raise us. Everybody pitched in.

There was a fund set up at the bank, and every pay-day people donated a little to provide for us financially so the costs of raising three extra kids wasn't a hardship on any one family.''

"And where did you all live?"

"Our house was mortgaged so it had to be sold and after that we lived pretty much nomadically. I know that sounds not much better than being shuffled between foster homes, but it really wasn't bad. We knew everybody and everybody knew us so we weren't going into strangers' homes. Plus we were never treated like burdens by anyone. One family would take us in for a while and then another would come along and say they'd like to have us and we'd go. I imagine it was prearranged, but as far as we knew, we were like the trophy that folks were vying to have a turn at keeping at their place. And wherever we were, we were treated like part of the family.''

"So you paid the town back by moving Tarlington Software here when they needed it and single-handedly brought new life to the place. Apparently, they made a good investment when they raised you,'' Paris said, admiring not only the people of Dunbar who had gone to such trouble to keep the brothers together, but also admiring Ethan for coming back to take care of them when he could.

"Or maybe they just raised us right. Either way, I think it worked out for everybody,'' he said, only impressing Paris all the more because he wouldn't take his part of the credit.

"Does this party have anything to do with paying them back for what they did for you and your brothers?'' she asked to soothe her own curiosity about what was being celebrated so elaborately.

"The party serves a couple of purposes. We hold it every year on the week of our parents' joint birthdays and their wedding anniversary—they always got a big kick out of sharing the same birthday so that was also the day they chose to be married. We do the party in remembrance of them, but it's also like a gift we give to the people who put a lot of time and energy and money into raising us. I guess you could say it's a thank-you to all of our parents collectively.''

"It's a pretty spectacular affair,'' Paris said, unable to hide the awe that was mounting in her with every new thing she learned about what the event would entail. "I can't quite believe the scale it's on.''

"Spectacular—that's a good word for it,'' he said as if it really did please him. "That's what I aim for every year. I want it to be a spectacular reward for all that was done for us.''

"Mountains of caviar. Beef, veal, pheasant, lobster, soft-shell crabs, shrimp, salmon aspic. The finest champagne. Gold-dusted fondant frosted cake filled with French custard. Truffles—the mushroom kind and the chocolate kind. A full greenhouse worth of flowers. Five hundred strings of lights. A violin quintet coming in from Vienna to play during the meal. An orchestra for dancing afterward. An hour-long fireworks display—just to name a few of the things you have planned? I think spectacular might be an understatement.''

Ethan just smiled.

And Paris was struck all over again by how great-looking he was.

Only, now that she knew something of his history, now that she knew he was the kind of man who paid his debts and looked after people who had looked after him, it was as if there was a new depth to his handsomeness that she hadn't seen before. A level of maturity and responsibility that was very sexy.

And then, too, they'd both finished their sherry and the liquor had gone straight to her head, strengthening her responses to him, which could also have been a contributing factor.

But either way she thought that she should put an end to the evening before something as simple as the blink of his eyes drove her to jump into his lap.

Ethan seemed to realize their glasses were empty just then, too. He held up his and said, "Another?"

Paris shook her head. "No, thanks. In fact I was just thinking that I should call it a night. As you discovered this morning, Hannah is not a late sleeper."

"Neither am I."

"I gathered as much," she countered pointedly.

"Was I out of bounds to go in there this morning?"

"No. But you don't need to worry that she isn't being taken care of. I always hear her and I know just about how long I can snooze before she gets irate and wants some attention."

"I didn't think you neglected her," he said as if he meant it.

"Good, because I don't."

"How about if I got her up a morning or two and let you sleep in?" he offered then, out of the blue and surprising her.

"Oh, I don't think that would be a good idea."

"Why not?"

"She's usually drenched and hungry and—"

"So I'd change her and feed her."

"Thanks, anyway, but I enjoy our mornings." And she wouldn't enjoy having them taken over by the man she was most worried about taking over more than that.

She didn't even want to talk about it any longer. So she stood and returned her glass to the wet bar, saying along the way, "But if I don't get some sleep now I might be less likely to hear her when she does wake up."

Then Paris turned around again to say good-night, expecting to find Ethan where she'd left him.

But instead he was halfway to the door.

"If I can't talk you into staying up I guess I'll just have to walk you to your room then."

"I can find my way now. You don't have to."

"I do if I want five more minutes with you. And since you look the way you do in those pants and that shirt, I definitely want five more minutes with you."

He *had* noticed.

In fact, he was noticing right then as his eyes did a slow crawl from her bare ankles up to her face. And from his expression, Paris had no doubt he liked what he saw.

She only wished she didn't like that he liked what

he saw quite as much as she did. And that she wasn't so tempted to stay in that den with him to languish in the warmth of his gaze. And maybe in his arms, too...

"I really need to get to bed," she said before she gave in to her own temptations.

He smiled again, this time with a wickedness to it, as if she were inviting him along.

"Alone," she said before she realized he hadn't actually given her any overt reason to say that.

His smile widened to a grin, and she just knew he wasn't going to let that slide.

"Did I say anything about joining you?"

"No, but you were thinking it," she accused, deciding that since she'd gotten herself into this, she might as well bluff her way through it.

"Was I?"

"It looked like it."

"I looked like I was thinking about going to bed with you?"

How had she gotten into this? And how was she going to get out of it?

"Yes, you did," she said with more bravado than she felt at that moment.

"Maybe you just *thought* that was what I was thinking because that's what *you* were thinking."

"I was only thinking that your sherry made me sleepy."

"Uh-huh," he said as if he didn't believe it for a minute.

Intent on playing this hand right to the end, Paris sighed and shook her head as if she were merely exasperated with him. "I think I'll just say good-night."

"Not until I have my last five minutes," he reminded. "But just in the hallway," he added pointedly.

He opened the door for her then, and Paris decided that keeping her mouth shut was the best thing she could do for herself as she led the way out.

Ethan followed and fell into step with her.

But thankfully he let the previous subject drop and said, "So I think I have some making up to do."

"You've lost me."

"Well, I spent half the drive in from Denver on the cell phone. I stood you up most of today and then spent the ride home on the phone again. I want to make up for that."

"There's nothing to make up for. Employees have no expectation of undivided attention."

"Okay, let's say I'm making it up to me, then, for missing out on your company. Here's what I was thinking—I need to do some things with my brothers tomorrow in the daytime—"

"Which is good because I have work to do."

"So how about a picnic supper in the evening? You, me, Hannah and a dinner I'll have Lolly pack for us? It stays light late and it'll actually be cooler than trying to do it in the middle of the day, I think it's the perfect time for it."

"That doesn't sound very businesslike."

"No, it doesn't, does it? But let's do it anyway."

They'd reached her bedroom door by then, and when Paris glanced up at him she found a smile on his sensual lips, this one full of devilry as those luscious blue eyes stared down at her, searching her face, her own eyes.

And before she had time to think about it, she heard herself say, "All right," in a voice that was barely more than a whisper, as if then her better judgment wouldn't hear.

That made Ethan's smile even broader, and Paris seemed to get lost in it. In that smile and those eyes and in the scent of his aftershave all around her and just in his presence—big and tall and muscular and all man...

He was going to kiss her.

She didn't know how she knew it but she did.

And she was going to let him. Even though she knew without a doubt that she shouldn't.

He came closer.

He leaned in.

She tilted her chin ever so slightly.

And then he did it. He kissed her.

On the cheek.

"I'll let Lolly know about our picnic," he said as he stepped back afterward. "Have a good night's sleep."

It took Paris a moment to realize what had happened. A moment in which she just stood there, stunned and a little embarrassed that that tilt of her chin might have let him know she'd expected more. That she'd wanted more. That she would have accepted more.

Then she got hold of herself, straightened her shoulders like a soldier standing for inspection and said a brisk, "Good night," before slipping into her room and leaving him unceremoniously behind.

But the truth was, more than embarrassed that he might have known she was anticipating a real kiss, Paris felt her third wave of disappointment for the day.

And that was when it occurred to her that of the two of them, *she* was behaving a whole lot more *un*businesslike than he was.

He was spending time with his brothers. He was sitting a respectable distance away from her. Even that kiss on the cheek was something he might have given any acquaintance.

While she had been pining for his company all day and offended that he hadn't sat nearer to her in the den and waiting for a kiss on the lips at her door.

Which meant that she needed to practice what she preached. Beginning immediately, by putting a stop to that latest disappointment that was running rampant through her.

But getting rid of that disappointment was easier said than done. Because no matter how hard she tried, she couldn't seem to stop wishing he would have pulled her into his arms and kissed her smack-dab on the mouth.

And kept on kissing her until her toes curled and she couldn't remember what day it was.

Chapter Five

It was the Tarlington brothers' tradition to visit their parents' graves on the actual date of their common birthday and anniversary. That date fell on the following day.

Ethan had a blanket of flowers made for the occasion, and he and his brothers picked it up at the florist before they went to the Dunbar cemetery far on the outskirts of town.

After so long a time the visits each year weren't really sad so much as they were poignant. They followed no particular pattern. Sometimes one or two or all three of the brothers had something to say, as if the headstone were an intercom connecting them to their lost parents. Sometimes no one spoke. Sometimes Ethan, Aiden and Devon reminisced about something they remembered from when their folks were alive.

But always they decorated the graves. They wished their parents a happy birthday and a happy anniversary. And when they all felt ready to go, they each touched the marble headstone and then spent several miles of the drive back into town in silence, dealing in their own ways with the feelings that rose to the surface.

It was when that silent time had naturally passed and they'd begun to talk again that Ethan finally broached the question he'd wanted to ask his brothers since dinner the night before.

"So you've seen Hannah. What do you think about her?"

"I think we should have brought her out here with us today so Mom and Dad could see their first grandchild," Devon said without hesitation from where he sat in the back seat of Ethan's SUV.

"Her eyes are Mom's eyes and she has that same dimple when she smiles really big," Aiden added from the passenger seat.

"That's what I thought," Ethan said quietly, not sure where the confirmation of his suspicions left him now that he had it.

"Neither of you guys have ever donated to a sperm bank, have you?" he asked with a lame chuckle.

"Not me."

"Not me, either. You're not off the hook that easily," Devon joked just as lamely.

"The thing is, though," Aiden said more seriously, "I really like Paris. She seems like a genuinely nice person."

"Yeah," Devon agreed. "And she's great-looking and has a sense of humor, and she's easy to talk to. I can't figure out why she wouldn't tell you if Hannah *is* yours. Did you scare her off with talk about hating kids or something?"

"I don't hate kids," Ethan said. "But we did talk about having them the night we met." He shook his head. "I don't mean that the way it sounded. What I mean is that when she asked if I was married I said I wasn't and that I had too much on my plate to even think about a wife or kids, that I was building my business and devoting myself to that, and that there was no way I was even close to wanting a family anytime in the near future."

"Let me get this straight," Aiden said with a laugh. "She asked you if you were married—a simple question—and instead of a plain no, you told her about why you didn't want a wife and kids right now?"

"I didn't tell her all about it, no. I just wanted to be clear from the get-go. I'd only come off the Bettina mess a few months before that and I was a little raw about the whole subject."

"Still, Paris couldn't have known that you went overboard because of some other woman," Aiden pointed out. "She had to have believed you meant what you said—no wife and no kids, no way."

"And after that diatribe it's a wonder she let you anywhere near her."

"So maybe," Aiden said, "she's keeping the fact

of your fatherhood to herself because she believes—rightly so after what you told her—that there's no way in hell you'd *want* to know or want anything to do with being a parent even if you did.''

It was a theory Ethan had thought about himself.

But even hearing it from someone else didn't make it ring true to him.

''I don't think that's it. I just have this feeling that there's more to it. It's really like she doesn't want me to know.''

''Could it be that she's just waiting for the right time?'' Aiden asked.

''And what would be the right time? After I've fallen for her? Are you saying that maybe she's setting some kind of trap because she thinks I'd bow out of the picture if I knew Hannah was mine now? That Paris is pretending Hannah isn't mine and then when I'm in deep enough she'll tell me she is? That Paris is as conniving as Bettina, only with a different angle?''

''Talk about taking the ball and running with it in the wrong direction! No, that's not what I was saying. I was saying that maybe Paris is just waiting for a time that feels right. I didn't know you were so paranoid.''

''Maybe that was a little overboard,'' Ethan admitted. ''It's just that this whole thing is so damn frustrating. And aggravating. And confusing.''

''So, okay,'' Devon said then. ''When we talked about this before, you didn't want to ask Paris straight-out if Hannah is yours because you wanted to wait until you knew if we saw the same thing in

Hannah that you did. But now that we have, why not just confront Paris?''

''Because remember there was a second part to it,'' Aiden answered before Ethan could. ''He wants to understand the reason behind Paris not telling him Hannah is his. If that's the case.''

''Besides,'' Ethan added now, ''what if she just denies it, takes the baby and goes as far away from me as she can get? And then the only way I'll ever know for sure is to go to court and force paternity tests, and the whole thing will end up ugly and hurtful.''

''And you'll lose Paris,'' Aiden finished.

''I don't *have* Paris,'' Ethan said more under his breath than not.

''But you must be thinking along the lines of *wanting* her or you wouldn't care why she isn't telling you the truth or if you ticked her off by pushing the issue,'' Aiden persisted.

''Which means we were right from the start—you do like her,'' Devon concluded.

''That was always a given. I don't sleep with women I don't like.''

''I think there's more to it than that,'' Aiden said. ''I've been watching how you are around her. I don't think you just like Paris. I think she's gotten pretty far under your skin.''

''I'm glad to know I've been scrutinized,'' Ethan commented without conceding anything.

''Does liking the lady change your mind about doing the whole family bit?'' Devon asked.

''I don't know if I'd go that far,'' Ethan hedged.

"How far would you go?" This from Aiden.

Ethan took a deep breath and blew it out as if he were aiming for candles on a cake. "Don't ask me hard questions."

"Since you don't seem to have any answers maybe you should be grateful that Paris is giving you some time to get used to the idea and figure things out," Aiden suggested.

"Except that it's hard to be putting the moves on her the way he wants to with that hanging over his head."

Ethan laughed wryly at that. And the element of the truth it had to it.

"So what're you going to do?" Aiden asked.

"Wait and see," Ethan answered.

"And take a lot of cold showers in the meantime," Devon goaded.

But it was true.

Because no matter what was going on with Hannah, Ethan was as hot for Paris as he'd been the night they'd met. Hotter, actually. Hotter with each minute he spent with her.

And it was taking every ounce of willpower he could muster not to go after her with all he had.

It was just that he kept asking himself what would happen if he gave in to all the urges that were driving him to distraction and then found out later that Paris was just working some scam on him the way Bettina had.

There couldn't have been a better evening than that one for a picnic.

By six o'clock the sun was no longer beating down

with the intensity of midday. The sky was still a bright, cloudless blue, and even though it was over eighty degrees, it was a pleasant heat.

The wicker basket beside Hannah in the back seat of the SUV Ethan was driving was filled with fried chicken, potato salad, deviled eggs, fresh fruit and brownies, and in a cooler on the floor was a bottle of chilled wine.

They didn't have far to go from the house to be out in the country, but when Ethan pulled off the road and headed for the location he'd picked out, Paris could see that it was the perfect spot.

There was a huge, ancient oak tree near a quietly babbling brook. Lush green grass grew as far as the eye could see, and several guernsey cows grazed only a few yards in the distance.

"We're having dinner with the cattle tonight, huh?" Paris joked when Ethan parked the SUV near the tree.

"We were invited and I just couldn't refuse," he joked in return. "But they must be good company because my brothers wanted to tag along and I had to put my foot down to get them to stay home."

"They could have come," Paris was quick to say. Actually she'd been warring with herself all day, knowing it would be safer if Ethan ended up asking Aiden and Devon to join them, hoping he didn't and knowing she shouldn't be hoping any such thing.

"You could call them on your cell phone right now and tell them to come if you want," she said, continuing the war by hoping he wouldn't and knowing she shouldn't have that hope.

Ethan had turned off the engine by then and he leaned over to say confidentially, "I didn't want them. I wanted to be alone with you. And Hannah."

A ripple of delight rolled all through Paris at that but she tried not to acknowledge it.

Not that it was easy not acknowledging anything that the man did to her. Especially when she'd been so exquisitely aware of every detail about him since the moment she'd laid eyes on him tonight.

He was wearing a pair of age-faded jeans that fitted him like a familiar lover's caress. A yellow short-sleeved mock-turtleneck T-shirt that hugged his broad shoulders, his hard chest and his bountiful biceps. His hair fell in finger-combed disarray that made her own hands want to run through it. He was freshly shaved and smelled of that intoxicating aftershave he wore. And it was definitely difficult not to acknowledge just how much she liked the whole package. Just how much it made her feel all feminine inside.

Of course, it didn't hurt that after changing her clothes three times in anticipation of this simple picnic she'd settled on about the most feminine thing she owned to wear—a wispy white, ankle-length sundress and strappy sandals.

"They liked you, though," Ethan was saying, the sound of his voice reminding her to pay attention to something more than the way he looked and smelled and made her feel.

"My brothers. Aiden and Devon liked you," he

clarified as if her expression had led him to believe she didn't know who he was talking about.

"I liked them, too," she answered, still sounding a little dim.

But Ethan let it pass and got out of the SUV.

"I brought rope," he said as he opened her door for her. "I thought I'd hang Hannah's car seat from the tree so she'll have a swing."

"She ought to like that," Paris said as she got out, appreciating that he'd thought of it and was willing to go to the trouble.

But nothing about setting up their picnic site seemed to be trouble for Ethan. Which surprised Paris a little.

It almost seemed strange that a man of his means, who even had his car driven for him when he chose and certainly didn't have to bother with any of the mundane day-to-day chores of life, was willing to spread a blanket on the ground for her and leave her to fish out Hannah's dinner from the diaper bag while he unloaded the rest of the car. Certainly Jason—who had considered laying out his own clothes to be beneath him—would not have done it, let alone volunteered to rig a swing for Hannah.

"I thought we could have some wine while you feed Hannah, play with her awhile, and then eat our own supper later on. Does that sound all right?" Ethan asked as he uncorked the bottle.

"Sounds fine," Paris said when, in fact, it sounded great.

"Can we prop her up against something so I can

work with the car seat?'' he asked as he handed Paris one of the two glasses of wine he'd poured.

"Sure."

She positioned the diaper bag so that it braced Hannah at approximately the same angle she would have been in the carrier.

Then, as Ethan went to work with that and the rope, she opened the jars of Hannah's food and began to spoon the strained carrots and peaches alternately into her daughter's mouth.

But as she did, her focus was actually less on the baby than on Ethan.

She told herself she just wanted to make sure he was securing the seat in a way that it would be safe. But the truth was she couldn't unglue her eyes from the sight of Ethan himself as he tossed the rope over a high branch and then worked with it until it cradled the seat.

He really did have a body to die for. He was tall and tight and lean and muscular. And without warning, watching him now gave her a sudden flash of the way it had felt to lie naked against him; her bare flesh pressed to his; those long, powerful legs entwined with hers; his strong arms holding her; the satiny heat of him all around her....

Hannah protested just then and Paris realized belatedly that she'd let too much time lapse between bites. Feeling guilty for that, she readjusted her focus.

But apparently the baby's complaint had drawn Ethan's attention, too.

"Everything okay?"

"Fine," Paris answered in a voice that had a

squeak to it as she forced her gaze to remain on Hannah so she wouldn't be distracted again.

"I think we're all set," Ethan said then. "See? I think it would even bear my weight."

Paris had no choice but to glance at him again as he demonstrated how sturdy the swing was by pushing down on it with all his might.

"Looks like it," she responded, making sure her voice didn't give her away a second time.

Then Ethan joined her on the blanket, sitting beside both her and Hannah.

"So how was your day?" he asked then, picking up his glass and tasting the wine Paris had forgotten about.

"Fine, dear. How was yours?" she said as if she were reciting a line from a 1950s sitcom, because that's what his question had sounded like.

Ethan laughed and played along. "Oh, you know, just a day at the office."

But Paris switched gears then and gave him a real answer to let him know that she was doing what little she'd been hired to do. "I had it out with your New York chocolatier. He was dragging his feet about sending the truffles in the heat. He wanted to charge more for sending them overnight delivery in an insulated container that would keep them from melting. But I brought it to his attention that there was already a provision for both the fast delivery and the dry ice containers in the contract, at the contracted price. So the truffles should be here tomorrow."

"Great."

"I also finally convinced the liquor distributor that

they did, indeed, short the champagne order by six cases. Those will be here tomorrow, too. And other than that, everything is under control and, so far, right on schedule.''

"That's what I like to hear.''

Paris was curious about how he'd spent his day since there had been quiet mutterings throughout the house staff about whatever it was he and his brothers were doing. But she didn't feel free to just ask outright, so without taking her eyes off Hannah, she said, ''Did you and your brothers do something fun?''

''Not fun, no,'' he said before drinking more of his wine.

For a moment Paris thought that might be all he was going to say.

But then he went on. ''Today is the real day of our parents' birthdays and anniversary. We always visit their graves.''

''Oh,'' she said, unsure what else to say and sorry she'd brought it up.

But Ethan didn't seem to be. ''When you lose your folks as young as we were, it's easy to…I don't know, not forget them exactly, but the memory fades. And with so many other people taking their place, we like to do this one thing every year to keep them a part of us, I guess. Or to let them know we *haven't* forgotten them, maybe.''

''That's really nice,'' Paris said quietly, touched by the fact that the brothers took pains to honor the parents they'd lost.

''What about you?'' Ethan said then, lightening

the tone somewhat. "I met your mom, but is your dad still living?"

Paris shrugged. "I don't know. He came home from work one day when I was five, announced that he wanted a new life, and that was the last Mom or I ever saw or heard from him again."

"Wow. I'm sorry."

"It definitely wasn't a nice thing to do. It also wasn't nice that he didn't pay child support. That made it really hard on my mom and that's why she's a little freaked out that I chose to have and raise a baby on my own. But in a way I think Mom and I are closer because my father was out of the picture, and I've always seen that as the up side."

"So you have a precedent in your family for single mothers."

"I've never thought of it that way, but I suppose we do."

"Is that how you envision your relationship with Hannah—closer than it would be with a dad in the picture?"

For some reason that question felt as if it held more weight than anything else they'd been talking about and Paris wasn't sure why.

She glanced up from feeding Hannah to look at Ethan and found a very serious expression on his face, but she still didn't understand the reason for it.

She answered him anyway. "I didn't have Hannah on my own just for that purpose. But yes, I hope she and I are as close as my mom and I are."

"Didn't you miss having a father in your life?"

"Here and there. But not so much that it was a

huge thing to me that there wouldn't be a father around when I made the decision to have Hannah. For me, fathers are like dessert—nice to have. But I survived without one and I think I turned out pretty well. I know I'm none the worse for wear because my father wasn't around. I have to believe that Hannah won't be, either.''

Of course the whole time Paris was saying that, Hannah was grinning a toothless grin at Ethan as if he were the most wonderful thing she'd ever seen.

He noticed it at about the same time Paris did and grinned back at her the same way, letting her hang on to one of his index fingers.

''I don't know,'' he said pointedly, ''I think fathers are pretty important.''

''All I'm saying is that I did okay without one. And apparently so did you.''

''I may not have had my own father, but I had a lot of male role models.''

Paris laughed. ''Do you think Hannah is going to need to learn how to be a man?''

''She might need to know how to relate to one.''

Paris glanced from him to her daughter, who was trying to get his finger into her mouth while still grinning at him. ''She seems to know how to do that naturally. Besides,'' Paris added, ''it isn't as if she'll be sheltered from all men. I have male cousins and friends and neighbors. The world is full of your kind,'' she ended with another joke.

''My kind?'' he repeated with a laugh.

Paris just smiled.

"Are we done eating strained stuff here?" he asked then, nodding toward Hannah.

Paris offered the baby another spoonful of fruit but Hannah wasn't interested.

"Looks like it."

"Then *my kind* wants to introduce her to the cows."

"Now that *is* a *your kind* kind of thing. Are you sure they won't bite or charge or something?"

"I'm sure. And it's something *my kind* knows."

"Ah, cows are a man thing. I was wondering," Paris said, going along with the joke he didn't seem to want to let die.

She wiped Hannah's face, and before she could say more, Ethan stood and picked up the baby.

"You're welcome to come, too," he invited, holding out his free hand to help her up.

Paris had every intention of going, and it seemed rude not to accept his help. It was just that of all the things she was trying not to acknowledge, the sparks his touch set off in her were harder to ignore than the rest all put together.

And the fact that once she was on her feet she didn't want him to let go? That she wanted him to go on holding her hand?

Not a good thing.

But he did let go, and that, too, was a problem for Paris, because when he did she felt that same disappointment rampant in her the day and evening before.

It just wasn't easy being with him, she decided. And she might as well accept that and ride it out.

Of course it wasn't easy *not* being with him, either, because then all she did was think about him and *want* to be with him.

But it's only this week, she told herself as they headed across the meadow in the direction of one of the guernseys. Just this week, and then they'd go their separate ways.

Yet somehow that thought wasn't altogether good, either.

But this wasn't the time to analyze it, she thought, letting herself off the hook. She was on a picnic. It was a beautiful evening. And there was nothing she could do about any of it, anyway, except try not to think about it.

"This is Betsy," Ethan said as they drew near the big brown-and-white animal.

Betsy had a mouthful of grass she was working on with a back-and-forth motion of her lower jaw, and she eyed them without much interest.

Hannah was thrilled, though. She was waving her arms as if she might take wing, and making sounds Paris had never heard her make before.

"Want to pet her?" Ethan asked the baby as if Hannah could answer.

He held her close enough so that one of her hands came into contact with the side of the cow's neck.

Betsy flicked an ear as if to shoo away a fly, and Hannah let out a squeal of delight.

"I think you might have to bring one of these home with you," Ethan said to Paris over Hannah's head as Hannah leaned forward to let him know she wanted to feel the cow again.

"I could be wrong but I think there are ordinances against keeping cows in the backyard."

Ethan set Hannah on the animal's back, keeping hold of her.

Hannah liked that, too, and kicked her legs as enthusiastically as she was flailing her arms.

Betsy turned her head in slow motion to eye the activities and then exhibited her displeasure by doing a leisurely stroll away from them.

And that seemed to be it for Hannah's introduction to cows.

They took a walk through the meadow from there, with Ethan carrying Hannah and regaling Paris with stories of adolescent antics he and his brothers and friends had pulled in this same countryside.

Then they wound up sitting beside the brook so Ethan could dip Hannah's feet in it—but only after clearing it with Paris and assuring her the water had been tested and it was free of unsavory organisms or bacteria.

He taught Paris how to skip rocks and teased her with threats to throw her in. And as the evening passed Paris began to remember one of the reasons she'd liked him so much that first night they'd met. Without the cell phone interruptions, without other people vying for his attention, Ethan was extremely good company. He was calm and intelligent. He was interesting and knowledgeable. He was interested in anything she had to say. He could be very funny. And it was just nice to be with him.

Something she almost wished she hadn't been reminded of.

The lower the sun got in the sky, the heavier Hannah's eyelids seemed to get. Paris had come prepared for that and laid her daughter on the blanket to change her diaper and put on her pajamas.

As she did, Ethan tickled Hannah's chubby cheek with a blade of grass, and when Paris was finished he asked if he could give Hannah her bedtime bottle.

Paris hesitated. That last cuddle of every day was one of her favorite times, and she didn't like relinquishing it to anyone. But seeing Ethan with Hannah since they'd arrived at their picnic site had done something strange to her and she discovered in herself the slight inkling to let him do it. To see him hold his child that way.

So, even though a part of her was against it, she let that other part rule just this once and agreed.

And it was something to see. Ethan leaned back against the tree trunk, and Hannah looked so safe there against his massive chest, so protected, so right.

And as the tiny baby gazed up into his face with fascination and accepted the bottle he offered her, the image of the two of them together gave Paris such a twinge that for the first time in fourteen months she felt a tiny, tiny urge to tell him he was Hannah's father.

But she shied away from it in a hurry.

"How did you get so good at handling babies?" she asked to distract herself from her own thoughts, her own unwanted inclinations.

"One of the families my brothers and I stayed with when we were kids had a baby Hannah's age. A boy.

I was about fourteen—old enough to baby-sit—so that became my job.''

"Did you like that?"

He laughed. "No, I wasn't thrilled with it. But it wasn't as if we went into these homes as guests. Everybody thought it was important to teach us things along the way the same as they taught their own kids—life skills, table manners, right from wrong. And we had chores everywhere we went, like taking out the trash or cleaning the garage or helping out around the house.''

"And in this particular house you were the baby-sitter?"

"It wasn't as if anyone took advantage of us. But, yes, I did some baby-sitting there. Anyway, once I got over balking at what I considered a *girl's* job, it wasn't so bad. Well, the diaper changing was—I never liked that. But I had some fun with the rest of it and, like a lot of what my surrogate parents taught me, you never know when it might come in handy.''

Hannah had finished her bottle and was still staring up at Ethan as if she were mesmerized by him.

He stood and set her in the baby carrier, strapping her in. Then he nudged it gently, putting the make-shift swing into motion and staying there to keep it going as she fought sleep to keep watching him.

But she could only fight it for so long, and she finally dozed off, freeing Ethan to join Paris on the blanket so they could eat.

"It seems like you've had an amazing number of good people in your life," Paris said.

"I have. All but one, actually.''

"That sounds very ominous." Not to mention intriguing. "Man or woman?"

"Woman."

"Someone who took you guys in as kids?"

"No, she came into my life three years ago."

"Ah. A romantic interest?"

"A romantic interest," he confirmed just as he was taking a bite of potato salad. But rather than soothing Paris's growing curiosity, when he could go on he said, "But that's not a picnic story. I don't want to ruin this with that."

Another bite of the creamy, spicy dish interrupted their conversation and when he'd finished it he said, "Besides, that's enough about my past for one day. Let's talk about your future."

"Are you going to make me a job offer?" Paris joked because of the way he'd worded that.

"I wasn't, no. But I could. Want to design my packaging or my advertising copy or my brochures? Or you could do something else. You could write your own ticket."

She wasn't sure if he was joking in return or not. "Are you playing fairy godfather?" she asked with a laugh.

"Is that what you want?"

Why did that sound like a test?

Paris just laughed again. "What I want is to paint. And raise my daughter."

"Alone."

"I don't know that I *want* to raise her alone. It's just the way things are."

"Does that mean if the right guy came along you'd marry him?"

Was she mistaken, or was there a note of jealousy in his tone?

"Yes," she answered honestly. "If the right guy came along—"

"What would make him the right guy?"

She thought about it. And tried to block the image of Ethan from her mind's eye. "He'd have to be down-to-earth, kind, considerate, levelheaded, fun to be with, ethical, honest, compassionate, unselfish—"

"So if you found Mr. Perfect you'd marry him?"

"I'd consider letting him into Hannah's and my life, yes. I'm not antimarriage. That was your deal, as I recall, not mine."

Ethan's brow beetled as if she'd struck a note with that. "I had a conversation about that with my brothers today as a matter of fact. Did I give you the impression that I was antimarriage?"

"No, you didn't give me that *impression.* You told me straight out—no marriage, no family for you. You were too busy and more interested in work."

He flinched slightly. "I was just coming off that bad experience we were talking about tonight—"

"With the bad woman."

"With the bad woman. So I may have been a little...overly negative."

"I don't know, you seem pretty busy to me. And pretty work oriented. I can't see where you have time for a wife or kids."

They'd finished eating by then and he glanced around them, obviously taking in the setting sun and the cattle in the distance, and the brook nearby. And Hannah.

"I'm not busy now. I'm not working now," he pointed out.

Paris just laughed again. "Tonight. And for all of one week out of the year that so far hasn't been without work phone calls."

"That doesn't mean I couldn't make time for marriage and a family if I wanted them. I could always delegate."

"And become a laid-back mogul?" she teased.

"Maybe. Anything's possible."

"Are you telling me that now you've decided you want marriage and a family in *your* future?"

He arched his eyebrows and shrugged his shoulders, too. "Never know."

"And what you want, you make sure you get," she said somewhat under her breath.

"What does that mean?"

"Just what it sounds like. You're used to getting whatever it is you decide you want. So I guess if you decide you want a wife and kids nothing will stop you from going out and getting them."

"Don't most people go after what they want? You did, didn't you? You wanted a baby and so you went for artificial insemination to get one."

Okay, now they were venturing into territory Paris didn't want to be in.

Luckily the mosquitoes were coming out in force right about then, and Ethan slapping one away from his arm gave her an out.

"We'd better get going before the bugs decide to have baby for brunch."

Ethan didn't jump into action. He just went on studying her as if he thought if he looked closely enough he might see something he might not see otherwise.

But when Paris began to reload the picnic basket with the remnants of their meal, he finally stood, untied the car seat and put Hannah in the SUV, out of harm's way.

Then he came back to help Paris clean up, and as he did he said, "So how is it different for me to go after what I want than for anyone else to?"

Keeping her eyes on what she was doing rather than letting them meet Ethan's, she said, "It's different because you have so much money. People with a lot of money lose the concept that they *can't* have whatever they want, and they also have the means to go after what they want at all costs. Even if it hurts other people."

"Are you thinking that I'm going to buy a wife and kids?"

"I think this is something *I* don't want to talk about tonight."

She regretted that she'd let it be known just how raw a nerve this was to her. But since he respected her wishes not to continue discussing it and went on to small talk, she just let it lie.

In fact, he stuck to small talk for the entire drive home, so Paris thought the subject was completely dead and she relaxed again.

Back at his house Ethan carried Hannah and the

seat inside. Then he stood by, watching Paris carefully put her daughter in the crib, and followed her out of the room into the hall when she had.

"I wanted to call my mom tonight and see how she's doing," Paris said then. "So I should say goodnight and do that before it gets too late."

But again Ethan didn't seem inclined to move from that spot just outside Hannah's closed door any more than he'd been in a hurry to leave their picnic blanket earlier. He remained standing there, looking down at Paris, searching her face yet again just the way he had then.

"I'm really not all work and no play, you know," he said with a crooked smile. "And I can't imagine ever using money to gain a wife or kids—if that was even possible."

"Whatever you say," she said, not thrilled to have the sore subject brought up again.

"If I was all work and no play I wouldn't have enjoyed tonight as much as I did."

"It was nice," she admitted.

He still didn't budge, though. He went on studying her with those blue eyes that were so intense Paris knew no color on her palette could do them justice.

And as much as she didn't want them to, those eyes drew her to him as if they were casting a spell over her.

"There's a dinner and dance tomorrow night at the church in town," he said then. "It's sort of in honor of me and Aiden and Devon. Will you go with me? As my date?"

"Oh, I don't know if that's such a good idea,"

she said in reaction to the word *date,* even as a little voice in the back of her mind said, *And what was tonight if not a date?*

"I think it's a great idea," Ethan persisted.

Paris shook her head, but before she could say anything, he said, "Come on. I want to be there with you. I want you to be there with me. No games."

All the reasons why she shouldn't do that were like a chorus in her head. But it was just background noise as Ethan's eyes held hers, as the power, the potency of the man himself seemed to engulf her.

"I shouldn't," she whispered, a denial that made it clear she was going to, anyway.

"Yes, you should."

"Hannah—"

"Can come along. There'll be a lot of kids there."

And then he did the one thing that put her completely over the edge. He touched her. He reached a big, capable hand to the side of her neck and rubbed it with the most tender brush of his fingertips as he said, "Say you'll come."

Paris thought she might have the weakest will of anyone in the whole world because that was all it took for her to say, "Okay."

It made him smile. A slow, pleased smile without a trace of self-satisfaction. Purely a smile that said she'd made him a happy man.

And then, as if it were perfectly natural, he bent over enough to kiss her.

Not merely a peck on the cheek like the night before, but a kiss in which his warm, sensual lips captured hers, parted over hers, lingered over hers and erupted memories in Paris that she'd been trying not to entertain. A kiss that reminded her how good he was at it. How much she liked it.

Then he ended it almost as unexpectedly as he'd started it and smiled down at her again. A smile that seemed to wash away the last fourteen months along with all the distance, all the formalities, all the barriers she'd tried to erect between them. A smile that took her back to a moment after they'd made love all that time ago, when they were both stripped bare literally and emotionally before each other.

"Good night," Ethan said then, sliding his hand away from her neck and leaving that spot feeling naked for the loss.

Paris didn't say anything at all. She just opened Hannah's door and slipped back into her daughter's room rather than move down to her own and risk that even another second of being without a physical barrier between herself and Ethan might make her completely incapable of leaving him at all.

But even once she was in the seclusion of Hannah's room, Paris knew she still hadn't really escaped.

Because what she wanted was to just go back out into the hall and throw herself into Ethan's arms.

So he could remind her of more than just how much she liked the way he kissed.

Chapter Six

"Let me hold her while you finish your lunch," Lolly offered.

Paris and Hannah were alone with the older woman in the kitchen the next day, and Hannah was fussy. Paris had hoped feeding her daughter would help, but it hadn't. Hannah didn't want to stay in her high chair and she kept wiggling around in Paris's lap, making it difficult for Paris to eat the egg salad sandwich Lolly had made her. So she didn't argue, she just handed Hannah over.

"Thanks. I don't know why she's so out of sorts today."

As the other woman bounced Hannah gently on her knee to occupy her, Paris finally gave in to curiosity and ventured the question she'd been trying not to ask since she'd come from working in the den and discovered she, Hannah and Lolly were dining alone in the kitchen.

"Did the Tarlington men jump ship?"

"They did. After breakfast the boys took off for town. Ethan has his work cut out for him with Dr. B."

Lolly said that as if Paris knew what she was talking about. Since she didn't, she said, "Dr. B.?"

"Bob Briscoe. He was the doctor around here until he retired about five years ago."

"Why does Ethan have his work cut out for him with Dr. B.?"

"The old dear is going blind and he just can't be living alone anymore. The trouble is he won't admit he needs help."

"He doesn't have any family?"

"His wife died about ten years ago and his daughter was killed in an accident last year, so, no, he doesn't have any family left. Except Ethan, Aiden and Devon—they consider themselves his family."

"Surrogate family? I know how they were raised, Ethan told me."

"We all like to think of ourselves as extended family. It sounds so much better," Lolly corrected. "Anyway, yes, Dr. B. and his wife took their turn having the boys live with them. In fact, I think it was because of Dr. B.'s influence that Aiden became a doctor."

Which still didn't explain why Ethan had his work cut out for him in regards to the man.

"Is Ethan hoping to convince him that he needs

help?'' Paris asked to remind Lolly of what they were talking about.

''I think he'll be doing a little more than convincing him. When Ethan heard about what was going on with Dr. B. he sent word from overseas to hire someone to live with him to take care of the house and look after him. Of course Ethan will pay for it— a country doctor doesn't get rich, and Ethan does things like that whenever a need arises around here. But poor Devon has been coming into town almost every week since then, trying to persuade Dr. B. to accept the help, and Dr. B. just keeps saying he doesn't want anybody in his house with him. No matter what Devon does, Dr. B. won't agree. He's a stubborn old cuss. Actually, he was a stubborn young cuss, too.''

''So what is Ethan going to do about it?''

Lolly slid Hannah down to straddle her shin, holding the baby's hands and giving her a horsy ride. ''He'll make sure it happens.''

''How will he do that if Dr. B. is so stubborn?''

''Ethan is more stubborn,'' Lolly said with a laugh.

Paris had taken a bite of her sandwich and she had to swallow before she said, ''You say that as if you know it for a fact.''

''I do. I had a hand in raising him, too, you know.''

Paris hadn't known that for sure but she'd assumed as much since Lolly acted more like a mother helping out around her son's home than like a housekeeper.

"And Ethan is even more stubborn than a stubborn old cuss?" Paris concluded.

"Maybe stubborn isn't the right word for Ethan," Lolly amended. "Determined might be better. Dr. B. is stubborn, but Ethan is determined, and Ethan is more determined than Dr. B. is stubborn."

"In other words, Ethan gets what Ethan wants."

Lolly laughed again and lifted Hannah back to her lap to bounce her there once more. "Ethan definitely gets what he wants. He'll steamroll Dr. B. if he has to. In fact, I believe the plan is to tell Dr. B. that Social Services has decided he's unable to live on his own and either accepts live-in help or he has to go to a nursing home."

"Is that true?"

"Not technically, no. But Ethan said that Dr. B. will have a live-in helper before he leaves there today, and I know *that's* true. Like I told you, Ethan is going to steamroll him."

Steamroll. Paris had never thought of what Jason did as steamrolling. Somehow that sounded a little friendlier than Jason's hiring a private investigator and a battery of lawyers and psychiatric experts who could slant their opinion whichever way he told them to.

But wasn't the end result the same? One person imposing his will on another?

Paris could feel her stomach tighten at just the thought.

"Does Ethan do a lot of steamrolling?" she asked.

"He does a lot of getting the job done."

"By steamrolling."

"By whatever means are necessary. Like I said, he's determined. But since old Dr. B. won't do what's good for him, what other choice is there? And it isn't as if Ethan won't keep Dr. B.'s wishes in mind. By the time Ethan is through, Dr. B. will end up with someone living with him, and the old stinker will think it was his idea all along."

For Dr. B.'s sake, Paris hoped Lolly was right. But whether or not she was, clearly she knew Ethan well enough to feel sure he would come out on top no matter what. And that served as a reminder to Paris that she shouldn't forget just how powerful a man he was. Which was certainly not what she'd been thinking about when she'd let him kiss her the night before.

"Poor Dr. B," Paris said more to herself than to Lolly.

"I know. We all feel bad for him," Lolly agreed, misinterpreting Paris's sentiments.

But Paris didn't correct the other woman's impression. She merely renewed her vow to herself to keep in mind who she was dealing with when she was dealing with Ethan Tarlington, that he was a man who always got what he wanted.

At any cost.

But by six o'clock that evening, when Paris was getting dressed to be Ethan's date at the dinner and dance in his and his brothers' honor, the last thing she was thinking about was that Ethan was a rich and powerful man she should be wary of.

She was just thinking about what to wear.

And how eager she was to see him again and the fact that a mere ten hours without seeing him felt like an eternity.

"I wish it was as easy to dress me as it is to dress you," she told Hannah, who was in the baby carrier on the floor of the closet dressing room.

Hannah had awakened from her afternoon nap in better spirits and was happily playing with her own feet in the tiny white shoes that went with her pink overalls and white T-shirt with pink rosebuds embroidered all over it. She looked adorable. But Paris was having more difficulty choosing something for herself.

She'd packed mainly work clothes, not date clothes, and even though she had a few dresses with her, they were the kind of dresses she'd have worn to a temp job in an office. The only exception was a slightly fancier, ankle-length, black jersey, mock-turtleneck dress that she'd included just in case she was invited to attend the party she was working on for Saturday night. But if she wore it tonight, she wouldn't have anything for Saturday.

Still, with no other options, she finally decided on the black dress for tonight. She would talk to Lolly about where in Dunbar she might buy something else if she did end up going to Saturday's affair.

The dress fitted her well, falling around her curves with just enough of a hug to accentuate them, and she wasn't sorry once she got it on. Then she slipped her feet into the black two-inch heels she'd brought to wear with it and grasped the handle on the baby carrier as if it were a basket of flowers to carry from the closet to the bathroom with her.

"You know I shouldn't be doing this," she told her daughter as she took special pains with her mascara and added a little eyeliner to her upper and lower lids. "I should never have accepted this being a date. This man has the potential to be a complication in our lives that neither one of us needs. A huge complication. A huge, huge complication. And if I had any sense at all, you and I would be staying right here in this room tonight, by ourselves. We wouldn't be going on a *date* with him."

Hannah made a cooing sound as if in answer, and even though Paris knew it was absolutely ridiculous, it was as if that sound soothed and reassured her that what she was doing, what she was looking forward to so much, was okay.

"I really am still trying to keep things cool with him," she continued as if justifying Hannah's imagined support. "And even though he said this was a date, it isn't as if it will be an intimate private date. We'll be in a public place, with probably the whole town there, too. It's completely innocent."

Her conscience called her a liar for that as she brushed a light clay-colored blush on each high cheekbone.

"Okay, so kissing him last night doesn't qualify as completely innocent. I know I shouldn't have done that. But there can't be any kissing going on at this dinner tonight. Not with him being one of the guests of honor and a lot of people around. So even if I did let things go further than they should have, this is still all right tonight because it's safe.''

Hannah giggled.

"Really," Paris said as if the giggle had conveyed the baby's doubts. "From here on I'll be more careful. I'm absolutely *not* going to let this get out of hand. I know what's at stake. Believe me, I know.''

Hannah made the soothing sound again, and again Paris felt better about what she was doing as she spun around to face her daughter.

"Well, what do you think? Not too bad?" she asked, referring to the finished product of her change of clothes, application of makeup and combing of her hair.

Hannah went into a paroxysm of excitedly flailing arms and kicking legs to accompany her toothless grin.

"I'll take that as a compliment," Paris said, hoping Ethan would be as enthusiastic, even as she warned herself that it shouldn't matter.

She picked up the baby carrier by the handle the way she'd done before and left the bathroom, pausing to give herself one last look in the full-length cheval mirror in the corner of the bedroom.

Satisfied with what she saw and knowing she was already five minutes late, she crossed to the door to leave.

"So, okay, here we go. Just a simple evening with a bunch of other people. No harm in that," she muttered as she stepped into the hall and headed for the formal living room where she was to meet Ethan.

All three Tarlington brothers were waiting for her

when she got there, but it was only Ethan she actually took note of.

He had on a pair of charcoal-colored slacks and a dove-gray dress shirt. He was freshly shaved, his hair was neatly combed back, and although there wasn't anything out of the ordinary about him, that one glimpse of him was enough for something purely sensual to skitter along the surface of Paris's skin and leave her with goose bumps.

"She cleans up nice, Ethan," Devon said loudly enough for Paris to hear, jabbing a teasing elbow in his brother's rib cage.

"I know," Ethan said with a rumble of appreciation in his voice and his eyes glued to her.

"You do look great," Aiden assured her without the note of machismo his brothers were batting back and forth. "And so do you, little Hannah," he added, bending over slightly to talk to the baby.

"Here, let me carry her," Ethan said, reaching to take the baby seat from Paris.

When he did, his hand brushed hers and set off a whole new wave of gooseflesh she was worried he might notice.

But if he did, he didn't comment on it.

Instead he said, "Are we ready to go?"

"If the diaper bag I packed earlier is still by the door, we are," she answered.

"Actually I already had it put in my car."

"Then I guess Hannah and I are ready."

Ethan nodded at his brothers and said, "See you guys there."

"I thought we might all be riding together," Paris

said, thinking that it would be better if that were the case and wondering if making the suggestion might inspire him to invite them along, after all.

But Ethan merely smiled a sly smile and said, "I haven't taken my brothers on my dates for a long time."

"Besides, he wants you all to himself," Devon confided.

"That, too," Ethan agreed, ushering Paris out of the house before anyone could say anything else.

His SUV was parked out front, and he secured Hannah's carrier to the back seat, flirting shamelessly with the baby the whole time.

And Hannah, as usual, flirted right back as if he were the greatest thing since strained plums.

Then Ethan opened the front passenger door for Paris.

She got in quickly, not giving him the opportunity to offer her help because she was afraid of what further contact with him might do to her.

But she couldn't help feasting on the sight of him as he rounded the front of the SUV, and that was all it took for a fresh outbreak of goose bumps.

She didn't know why she was having an even stronger reaction to him than normal. Her normal reaction to him was strong enough; she certainly didn't need it to get worse.

Then he got in behind the steering wheel and she caught a whiff of his aftershave and that only compounded it, leaving her almost desperate to find something about him to turn herself off.

Which was when she remembered her lunchtime conversation with Lolly.

"Did you persuade Dr. B. to have someone move in with him?" Paris asked as Ethan started the engine and pulled away from the curb.

He took his eyes off the road just long enough to cast her a curious gaze. "How did you know about Dr. B.?"

"Lolly told me what you were doing today."

Ethan drew his head back slightly on his shoulders and shot her another glance. "Why does that sound so accusatory? Did I do something wrong?"

"I don't know, did you?"

"I don't think so."

"Did you force him to have someone come in and live with him against his will?"

Ethan chuckled. "I persuaded him that that was what he needed or Social Services—called in by the hospital when he burned himself a few months ago because he couldn't see what he was doing at the stove—was going to make him go into a nursing home."

"But Lolly said that wasn't true."

"Well, not entirely. But Social Services assigned him a case worker who's been checking on him, and she's on the verge of passing down that mandate. I think the only reason she hasn't is that she lives here in Dunbar and has known Dr. B. her whole life. So I just fudged a little."

Like Lolly's steamrolling comment that made it sound so much better than what it actually was—a lie Ethan had used to accomplish what he'd set out to do.

"So you led him to believe he didn't have a choice."

"He thought he had the choice of going to a nursing home or having someone move in to help out."

"When he really still had the choice of living there alone the way he wants to."

This time when Ethan looked over at her he was frowning. "I introduced Dr. B. to Shirley McGillis. Shirley is a healthy, active seventy-five-year-old retired nurse who shares Dr. B.'s interests. And Dr. B. ended up more than happy to open his home to her by the end of today. Now, this not only serves Dr. B. It also works out for Shirley since her late husband gambled away all their retirement money and left her with so much debt she had to sell her house and was not only in need of a place to stay, but was going to have to go out and try to find a job again. So, if the truth be known, what I did today was solve two problems with what came out more as matchmaking than as forcing anyone to do anything, thank you very much."

That did put a better spin on it.

But then Paris couldn't help recalling that Jason talking about what *he* was doing had made him sound like a great guy, too.

Before she had a chance to say anything Ethan continued.

"Shirley and Dr. B. will be at this dinner tonight—something Dr. B. wasn't going to attend before because he was too proud to ask for a ride and he can't drive anymore. But Shirley can still drive and so now he has the advantage of mobility, again, too. And you can see for yourself if I did something bad today.''

''You manipulated two people's lives,'' Paris persisted, but it was getting more difficult to put any conviction behind it.

''I put two people together to the benefit of them both.''

''And if, down the road, Dr. B. decides he doesn't like Shirley or having her in his house? Is he going to believe his only other option is a nursing home?''

''I've known Shirley for a long time. She came in and took care of me just before she retired when I broke my leg in three places skiing. I've kept up with her over the years and I'm here to tell you Dr. B. will love her.''

''And if he doesn't?''

''I'll take care of it.''

They'd reached the Dunbar church by then—a white frame country chapel with a tall steeple—and once Ethan had parked in the lot beside it and turned off the engine, he draped his left forearm over the steering wheel and pivoted just enough to look Paris square in the eye.

''Are you mad at me for something?'' he asked, confusion echoing in his tone.

If only she were. It would have made things so much easier.

''No, I'm not mad at you. I just didn't like thinking that you were out forcing someone to do something against their will.''

"Not my style."

He held her eyes with his for a moment longer but then his brothers pulled up beside them and several other people also arrived, getting out of their vehicles to call to the brothers and approach them. It was clear Ethan and Paris couldn't stay sitting in the SUV.

But before Ethan let his attention stray, he reached over and took her hand, sending more goose bumps rippling up her arms.

"Can we just go in and have a nice time?" he asked with a smile so sweet, so charming, it felt like the sun's rays at the end of a cold winter.

And because of that and those goose bumps, Paris was afraid if she answered him, her voice would betray her, so she merely nodded.

Ethan squeezed her hand and then let go. "Good. Because that's what I was looking forward to tonight."

She melted a little more to know that she hadn't been the only one eager for their date and tried to recoup some of her determination to resist her attraction to him.

But it didn't help a whole lot, and as Paris let herself out of the car while Ethan opened the rear door and released Hannah's seat, she decided it was a good thing they wouldn't be alone tonight.

A very good thing.

The dinner was in the church basement. There was a long buffet table and several more tables set up around the perimeters of the big, open room, leaving

one corner for the live band and the center of the
floor free for dancing afterward.

It was surprising to Paris how many faces she already recognized even after being in town such a
short time. And not only was she recognized in return, but she and Hannah were both treated as
warmly as the Tarlingtons were.

Which was no small thing because Ethan, Aiden
and Devon seemed to be the darlings of Dunbar.

Lolly and the rest of the house staff were there
with their respective spouses and children so Paris
got to meet them all. The florist, the grocer, the
butcher, the baker and everyone else she was working with on the party couldn't wait to introduce her
to their families. The town's mayor was there, letting
her hair down as if she didn't have a political thought
in the world. Four of the five members of the police
force had come. The church minister, his wife and
six kids were there, and that was just who Paris
talked to the first hour.

By the second hour the room was brimming with
adults and kids and food and drink galore.

Lolly confiscated Hannah like a doting grandmother who wanted to show her off, leaving Paris
unencumbered as Ethan mingled and took her along
with him.

Not that she had any complaints. Ethan made sure
no one he spoke to went without meeting her and
learning a little about her. He included her in every
conversation and told her a little something about
each new person she met that made most of them
easy to remember.

All in all Paris was having a very pleasant time until they were approached by a woman named Honey Willis.

Ethan introduced Honey Willis as an old friend.

Honey amended the introduction to let Paris know she and Ethan had been a couple the entire way through high school—the *cutest* couple. That she'd been instrumental in getting him voted best kisser in their senior class, because, after all, who would know better than she. And that she'd been sure they would end up married to each other. Which could still happen since she was newly divorced and free to take up where she and Ethan had left off when Ethan had gone away to college.

Ethan treated the open come-on as if he didn't take her seriously, as if she were only teasing, but Paris knew she wasn't and she was reasonably sure Ethan did, too.

And although Ethan's touch did unsettling things to Paris's insides, she was glad when he draped an arm around her waist, excused them and took Paris to the buffet table to get something to eat.

Paris wasn't so glad, though, when, after dinner, Honey charged Ethan, grabbed his free hand and literally dragged him onto the dance floor for the first dance.

Lolly was nearby at the time and provided the distraction of pointing out to Paris that she'd changed Hannah into her pajamas and put the baby to sleep in the carrier on the chair beside her. But even that only kept Paris's eyes off the former high school sweethearts for so long.

Before she knew it she was watching them even as she tried to pretend she wasn't. And she saw it all. All five feet eight inches of slender, curvaceous blonde in Ethan's arms, smiling coyly at him, sensually massaging his biceps and shoulder, arching her back so her voluptuous breasts made themselves known at his chest.

And Paris was being eaten alive by jealousy, plain and simple. Jealousy that no amount of reasonable, rational thought could temper.

It seemed like the longest dance in the history of mankind. Paris didn't think it would ever end, and she wondered if, when it did, Honey Willis would have won Ethan over. If, when that dance ended, he might look at Honey with the warmth in his eyes that he'd reserved for Paris of late. If this date might take a turn for the worse in a way she hadn't anticipated.

And no amount of telling herself that it shouldn't make any difference to her if he rekindled his old romance or not calmed down the turmoil she was feeling as she watched them. No amount of telling herself that it would actually be great if Ethan rediscovered an interest in the other woman convinced her it was so. No amount of reminding herself that she didn't want him in her and Hannah's life made her not want to rush that dance floor and yank Honey Willis away by the hair.

The dance finally did end, but Honey didn't let go of Ethan immediately. Instead she kept hold of him and stood on her tiptoes to whisper something in his ear. Something that caused him to laugh that deep, rich, whiskey laugh that sent a fresh wave of jealousy through Paris.

But then he shook his head, reared back slightly and held up both hands—palms out as if he were warding off something.

Whatever Honey Willis had said—or suggested, or offered—he was apparently declining.

And some of Paris's jealousy ebbed at the sight.

Then Ethan pointed in Paris's direction as if he'd said he had to get back to her, and that was just what he did.

He came off the dance floor, straight to where Paris was sitting and stood behind her chair with both hands on her shoulders. Both big, strong hands taking her firmly in his grip and shooting a shock wave of electricity from there all the way through her. And even though she didn't mean to, she leaned into it.

"I just told Honey that I promised the rest of my dances to you," he said, bending to speak into her ear where the warmth of his breath only intensified her reaction to him. "Don't make a liar out of me."

Paris's spirits took quite a leap and she had to put some conscious effort into not letting her actions follow suit by jumping to her feet to dance with him.

Instead she gazed up at him and gave him a coy smile of her own. "What am I? Your protection?" she joked.

"Oh, yeah," he said with a laugh as he straightened up, abandoned her shoulders to reach for her hand and pulled her to her feet to take her to the dance floor.

''Keep the slow ones coming for a while, will you, Pete?'' he said to one of the members of the band.

Then he swung Paris into his arms, holding her just a little closer, she thought, than he'd held Honey.

But still, a small wedge of jealousy jabbed at Paris and before she even knew she was going to say it, she said, ''She was your first, wasn't she?''

Ethan didn't answer that for a moment. He just looked down into Paris's eyes.

Then he smiled a small smile and, in a voice for her alone, he said, ''You were my last.''

She knew she shouldn't have been so glad to hear that but she couldn't keep another smile from tugging at the corners of her mouth.

''Oh, you're good. You're very good,'' she said as if she thought he were only feeding her a line, not wanting him to know how pleased she'd been by his answer.

But he opted for misinterpreting her comment and putting a lascivious spin on it. ''I'm happy to hear you thought so.''

Paris suddenly lost all jealousy and with it a large portion of the reticence she'd been trying so hard to hold on to, and she just laughed.

''Did she proposition you?'' she asked as if she had the right to, amazed at the boldness that was coming from nowhere to spur her on.

''She did. But I turned her down. For some reason I haven't been interested in other women for the past fourteen months.''

''So I'm pretty good, too,'' Paris said, shocking

herself even more and making Ethan laugh again, this time heartily.

"Good enough to keep you on my mind ever since."

"Guess I should have been voted best kisser, too, then."

"You get my vote, that's for sure. Best kisser. Best everything. I'm just not sure what makes you so touchy about some things," he added as if he were confiding a secret.

"Who me? Touchy?" Paris responded as if she couldn't imagine what he was talking about.

Ethan pointed his well-defined chin toward where the old town doctor was dancing with his new companion.

"Dr. B. and Shirley McGillis," he said as if she needed reminding who they were even though he'd made a point of introducing her to them. "They look like they're enjoying themselves, wouldn't you say?"

"Mmm," Paris said noncommittally.

"So why were you so touchy about them earlier?"

"I wasn't touchy about them. I just wasn't sure about you," she said, couching the truth in a tone that made it sound as if she were teasing.

"About me," he said, seeing through her.

Paris shrugged. "I know you're used to having things your own way and—"

"I wasn't getting my 'own way' here. I was trying to do what was in the best interest of Dr. B. and Shirley."

Paris had heard that before. She raised her chin in

silent affront despite the fact that the entire conversation was amiable.

"Why do I feel like this has roots in something else?" he asked then.

"Take my word for it, you don't want to talk about that now," she advised.

"I want to talk about anything that lets me know what makes you tick."

"It isn't something that makes me tick. It's just something I've seen before," she said, as if her past experience hadn't affected her almost as much as it had the people who had been in the middle of it.

"What have you seen before? Someone telling a little white lie to accomplish what was best for someone else?"

In the best interest of Dr. B. Telling a little white lie to accomplish what was best for someone else— Paris nearly flinched at all the phrases that were so much the same as what Jason had said to her about his own actions when those actions and what those actions revealed about the kind of person he was caused her to end it with him.

"I've seen someone misuse his power and position and money for what he said was in the best interest of others when the truth was, it was just to hurt another person and get his own way. To control things and people."

"Nice," Ethan said facetiously. "And who was this Machiavellian gem?"

"A man I was engaged to."

That made Ethan frown. "Was it you he hurt?"

"Not directly. But when I learned what he was

doing, what he was capable of, and saw how he could justify it to himself without any remorse whatsoever, I ended the engagement, which was painful for me, too. Just not as painful as what he was doing to someone else.''

"Which was what?''

It was so nice dancing with Ethan, being in his arms, basking in the heat of his eyes that Paris seriously considered not getting into this subject.

But then it occurred to her that maybe she should get into it exactly *because* she liked dancing with him so much, to keep herself in check.

So she said, "Jason—that's his name, Jason Hervay—had been married before and he had two kids with his ex-wife. He hadn't left her, she'd left him because—or so he said—she couldn't take his long, erratic work hours.''

"What did he do?''

"He's one of the most prominent thoracic surgeons in Denver.''

"I thought surgeons kept pretty regular hours.''

"They aren't on call as much as other types of doctors, but there were more days than not when surgeries ran long or emergencies had to be dealt with, so there were still a lot of unpredictable hours. In the end I doubt that was really the reason, but before I found out what he was really like, I bought it.''

"I see.''

"Anyway, when I met him the marriage was long over, but the divorce proceedings were still dragging on. I found out later that that was all Jason's doing. Since he could afford to pay his lawyers indefinitely

and he knew it was a terrible strain on his ex-wife—
that was how he got what he wanted on every issue—
she'd eventually be forced to give in because she
needed the whole thing to get over with more than
he did. Then it came down to the custody of the
kids.''

"By then you were engaged to this guy?"

"I was. It was sort of a whirlwind romance. But
I had no idea what was really going on with the
divorce. He blamed his ex-wife for prolonging things
and I believed him. I wasn't involved in any of it,
the divorce wranglings were all handled by his lawyers. I only knew that Jason was charming and char-
ismatic and suave. That he was hard to resist. It was
only when he started to do what he did over the
children that his ex-wife reached the breaking point.
She came to the house one day to see him. To beg
him to stop. Only Jason wasn't there. I was. And she
ended up telling me what he'd been doing.''

"Which was what?"

"Just about every awful, underhanded, unethical
thing you can imagine. For instance, the fact that she
had to work two jobs to make a dent in her legal
fees translated into her neglecting the kids or abusing
them because she had to pick them up late from the
baby-sitter a night or two. The stress he was causing
her led to a doctor putting her on antidepressants—
that turned into her being an unstable drug user.
Bringing a male friend from her church in for coffee
one evening was twisted into lewd and inappropriate
behavior in front of the kids. The list just went on
and on. Jason had private eyes harassing her, follow-

ing her, following the kids, openly investigating everyone she or the kids came into contact with—the baby-sitter, his former in-laws, even one of her bosses—and Jason managed to find stones to throw at her in one form or another at every turn.''

"Wow.''

"I did some investigating of my own, after talking to her. According to Jason, of course, she was a horrible person, but she just seemed distraught to me. And I kept remembering a time or two when Jason had gloated over something that had happened with her and it hadn't sat well with me even before meeting her. So I talked to the kids, to the house staff members who had been there during the marriage, even to the wife of Jason's best friend. And what I discovered was that his ex-wife had been telling the truth—she wasn't an unfit mother. In fact, she was a good mother and Jason was really just manufacturing—or paying other people to manufacture—most things against her.''

"So did you help her keep her kids?''

"I tried. I even testified in court that Jason had lied about her. But it just didn't do any good. Jason claimed that he'd broken our engagement—which wasn't true, either, I'm the one who did that—and that I was just trying to get even with him by siding with his ex-wife. The judge apparently believed that, too. Prestige goes a long way, after all. Jason was granted custody.''

"Well, at least you did what you could. There aren't a lot of people who would sacrifice their own relationship to help someone else.''

"It wasn't a sacrifice. Yes, I loved Jason—or thought I did before I found out what kind of person he really was. But not only did I not want a man who could do what he'd done, I looked at this ex-wife and I saw myself. I saw what could happen to me if things between us didn't work out. And it was terrifying."

"Did he take your leaving him in stride?"

"No. But luckily I didn't have the connections with him that his ex-wife did. He had introduced me to a gallery owner who was going to give me a career-launching showing of my work and that, of course, got canceled first thing. And for a while that gallery owner bad-mouthed me and I had some problems, but eventually it died down and there was nothing else he could do to me."

"How long ago was this?"

"I'd broken up with him about six months before I met you."

Ethan nodded, searching her expression for a moment before he said, "And how does this all compare to me arranging for Shirley to take care of Dr. B.?"

"You manipulated the facts, didn't you? You pressured Dr. B. You made up your mind how things should be for him and—"

"It was all out of necessity, which made it a *justifiable* manipulation of the facts," Ethan said, defending himself.

"Jason said what he was doing was justifiable, too. When I had it out with him, he said he could give the kids more, give them a better life than their mother, so it was all right that he'd exaggerated a few things or made things look worse than they actually were. The ends justified the means—that's what he said. But he was just getting even with his ex-wife for the audacity of leaving him, plain and simple."

"I wasn't getting even with anybody today, Paris. You can see for yourself that what I did was not a bad thing."

"It was still the strong overpowering the weak," she said softly.

"But it wasn't out of vindictiveness. There's a big difference there."

Okay, maybe there was a difference. But still Paris knew she had to be leery. "I'm just saying that a person with money and power behind them can do damage to other people's lives."

"And you were just looking out for the underdog today in case I was running amok."

Paris shrugged again. "It's a sore spot with me."

Ethan stared at her for a moment before he said, "You know, money and power notwithstanding, some people can take it on the chin. Not everyone has the need to destroy the person who hurt them."

There was something in his voice when he said that that caused Paris to look more closely at him. "Are you speaking from experience now?"

He smiled down at her again. "Maybe. But that really *is* a story for another time. In fact, I'm thinking I should have taken your word for it about this one and left it out of tonight. What do you say we call an end to the debate and just dance, like the old cuss who got me into trouble today?"

This time it was Paris who nodded in the direction of Dr. B. and Shirley McGillis who had returned to one of the tables surrounding the dance floor.

"They aren't dancing anymore," Paris said, just to be contrary.

"But we are. So let's just enjoy it." He leaned to speak into her ear again. "We are supposed to be on a date here, remember?"

She couldn't argue that. Especially not when, despite what they'd been talking about, she was enjoying dancing with him.

"Okay," she agreed.

That was all Ethan needed to pull her even closer. So close she had to rest her head against his shoulder.

And that was how they stayed through two more dances, just swaying together, holding each other, oblivious to anyone else in the room.

Until Devon called from the sidelines to the band, "Enough of this slow stuff. Can't we shake it up a little?"

The band leader Ethan had told to keep playing slow songs looked to Ethan. "What do you say?"

"I guess if you have to," Ethan agreed reluctantly.

And with that go-ahead, the band broke into some hard core rock and roll.

"Think Hannah will sleep through this?" Ethan asked as he and Paris stopped dancing, his voice raised to be heard over the din.

"Not for long," Paris shouted back.

"Then let's get her out of here."

It seemed perfectly normal for Ethan to take her hand and lead her off the dance floor. Not so perfectly normal to keep hold of it as he picked up the baby carrier with his other hand and they said their goodbyes, but nice all the same.

So nice that Paris hated it when he had to let it go once they reached the SUV and he needed both hands to strap in Hannah's seat.

On the short drive back to the house they talked about the dinner and the people there, and then paused to put Hannah to bed so their voices didn't disturb the silence of her room.

But once the baby was tucked in, Ethan surprised Paris by taking her hand again to pull her out of the room into the hallway.

"I don't suppose you'd have a nightcap with me even if I asked, so I won't," he said when he had her there with Hannah's door closed behind them.

Actually, tonight Paris thought she might have accepted. But since he wasn't asking, and spending the evening in his arms had already pushed her willpower to the limits, she didn't tell him that. She merely let him believe he was right.

He went on holding her hand, though, raising it to study her fingers as he said, "But I want to talk to you about tomorrow. We need to go into town about four o'clock tomorrow afternoon. Just you and me."

"Oh?"

"I can't tell you why. But I've set it up with Lolly to baby-sit Hannah. I thought we'd stay and have dinner there, too. Just you and me. Will you do it?"

"Is this for work?"

"Nope."

His complete lack of subterfuge made her laugh. "Is this another date?"

"In between."

"In between," she repeated, having no idea what that could mean. "And you can't tell me what the trip into town is for?"

"Well, I *could* tell you. I just don't want to. I want you to see when you get there. So what do you say?"

Her curiosity was intense. Almost as intense as his charm and her desire to spend the next evening with him. Alone. "I suppose it would be all right," she finally agreed, fully aware that she was giving in to temptation when she shouldn't be.

"I hope it'll be better than all right," Ethan countered. "Like tonight. I had a great time tonight. Even if you do think I might be as big a jerk as that other guy," he joked.

"Did I say that?" Paris joked in return.

"What about you? Did you have a good time?" he asked, running his thumb over her knuckles in a slow, barely-there sweep, back and forth.

"You mean did I have a good time even if you did have your old high school sweetheart hanging all over you?"

He chuckled at that one. "Yeah, even though we both had some history intervening, did you have a good time tonight?"

"I did. How could I not have when I was with Dunbar's best kisser?"

He used his grip on her hand to pull her nearer, looking into her eyes. "Well, that's true," he said with a devilish smile and a low, intimate voice.

"And now that you have me alone you should probably avail yourself of my talents."

Paris laughed but somehow it came out a more breathy, sensual laugh than she'd intended. "I don't know about that."

"I do," he responded with confidence just before he leaned in enough to press his lips to hers.

At first it seemed as if it would be a quick kiss, and Paris was all ready to tease him about it not being up to best-kisser standards. But then, rather than ending it after only a few moments the way he had the kiss the night before and giving her the opening, he deepened it.

His lips parted over hers and hers parted in purely unconscious response as he released her hand and wrapped his arms around her in a way that made holding her on the dance floor nothing at all.

One hand cradled the back of her head, the other supported her back against a kiss that could have won him the world title for best kisser as his tongue traced the tips of her teeth and came to say a sexy *hello* to her tongue.

All on their own Paris's hands slipped under his arms and around to his back where she could feel the hard strength of muscle and tendon honed to perfection.

She knew she shouldn't be doing this. But she just couldn't deny herself that moment of pleasure.

And pleasure it was. Pleasure that sent a raging river rushing through her, tightening her nipples into solid nubs against his chest, bringing every nerve ending to the surface of her skin, heightening her

awareness of everything about him—his wonderful
scent, the heat of his breath on her face, the perfect
pressure and enticement of a kiss to wash away all
thought, the way his body cupped around hers pro-
tectively and seductively all at once, the feel of his
solid back beneath her hands...

But for some reason she didn't understand, she
suddenly started to think about what they'd talked
about on the dance floor. About Jason. And the in-
trusion of the past into that kiss reminded her why
she really shouldn't be doing what she was doing.
Why she really did have to stop it.

She pulled her arms back and pressed her hands
to a chest so glorious her palms ached to stay pressed
to it, to explore it.

But that wasn't what she did. She forced herself
to push slightly against him even as she drew away
from his kiss.

"Okay, okay, you get my vote, too," she said,
trying to make light of what had turned into much
more, and giving herself away with the huskiness of
her voice.

Ethan searched her face with his azure eyes and
he seemed to know why she'd stopped, because in a
very quiet voice, he said, "Do me a favor. Take a
good, long look at who *I* am without coloring it with
who he is."

She just lifted her chin at that. She couldn't comment because she was too lost in the warm depths of
his eyes.

But he must have taken her silence as agreement

because he smiled again and said, "Tomorrow at four."

Paris nodded. "I'll be ready."

Then Ethan leaned over and kissed her again. Softly. Sweetly. Gently. As if to leave her with that memory rather than the one that had brought Jason with it.

And it worked.

Because as Ethan said good-night and left her to go to her room, it wasn't her former fiancé Paris was thinking about.

It was Ethan. Only Ethan.

And how much she was craving more of that kiss she'd ended.

More of that kiss and more than kissing....

Chapter Seven

"What do we have here?"

Ethan had been out skeet shooting with his brothers for a good portion of the day and had returned home to clean up before taking Paris into Dunbar. But he altered his course when he passed by the entrance to the living room and spotted Lolly sitting on a blanket on the floor playing with Hannah.

"We have the cutest baby in the world, is all," Lolly answered, dangling a toy octopus over Hannah so Hannah could try grabbing the legs.

"Where's Paris?" Ethan asked.

"She's overseeing the tent being set up out back and working with your chef, who arrived a couple of hours ago to officially take over the kitchen, to make sure he has everything he ordered. Then she said she was going upstairs to get ready for her trip into town with you.''

''That's why I came home—to shower. But I think I can spare a few minutes,'' he said, joining them on the blanket.

''Hello, little Miss Hannah,'' he greeted the infant.

''Would you look at that smile! Does she love you!'' Lolly exclaimed with a laugh.

Lolly took the octopus out of his way, and Ethan held out both index fingers for Hannah to grab on to instead. Then he pulled her to her tiptoes.

''I think she wants to walk,'' Ethan said, feeling a rush of pride he still didn't know if he was entitled to. Or even *wanted* to feel.

Lolly must have heard something in his voice that opened a door for her because she said, ''She's yours, isn't she?''

''Why do you say that?'' Ethan hedged, letting Hannah bounce slightly and delighting himself and the baby.

''I was your mother's best friend, remember? We were closer than sisters from the time we were in diapers ourselves. I still have her photograph on my dresser. And every time I look at Hannah, I see her.''

Ethan had wondered about that. In fact, he'd wanted Lolly's opinion more than his brothers'. After all, his brothers had been even younger than he was the last time they'd seen their mother in person. But Lolly—Lolly had known their mother better than anyone.

''I didn't want to be the one to bring it up,'' Ethan

said by way of explaining why he hadn't said anything to her.

"Is it a secret?"

"From me. If it's true," he said with a wry laugh
and then some baby talk to answer the chattering
Hannah seemed to be directing at him.

"I don't understand," Lolly said.

"Join the club. I didn't even know there *was* a
Hannah until I paid Paris an impromptu visit last
Friday and discovered her. Paris says she had Han-
nah by artificial insemination."

"And you called me and had me put away all the
pictures of your mother before you got here so Paris
wouldn't see that anyone who took one look at Hannah would notice she's the spitting image of your
mom. I wondered why you wanted that done. This
is very strange, Ethan."

Ethan smiled at that. The comment itself and the
fact that the tone Lolly delivered it in sounded very
motherly, almost like one of the reprimands he remembered her giving when he was a kid.

"Hey, don't look at me," he answered, much the
way he would have years ago. "I'm supposed to be
in the dark, too."

He transferred his hands to Hannah's rib cage so
he could toss her gently in the air and catch her
again, making her giggle.

"Why?" Lolly asked.

"Paris couldn't very well explain why she's keeping a secret when she's still keeping it, could she?
So your guess is as good as mine."

"Do you think she has an angle? Like Bettina?"

"I don't know. I've wondered about that. I guess there's a part of me that's still wondering about it. But after last night I'm beginning to get another idea of what might be behind Paris pretending Hannah isn't mine. I'm thinking she might be afraid of me."

"Afraid of you? That's crazy."

"I don't think it's crazy to her." In fact, it explained why she seemed so protective of Hannah when he'd first seen the baby. "I'm just hoping she'll get over it."

"Do you want me to talk to her? We've gotten pretty friendly since she's been here."

"No, don't do that. Don't even hint about Hannah looking like Mom. I don't want Paris scared away, and that might do it."

"So you do like her—baby or no baby."

"You could say that," he said as if it were no big deal when the truth was it was a very big deal. The biggest deal, and it was getting bigger all the time, no matter how hard he fought it. It was getting to be such a big deal that he couldn't spend five minutes not thinking about her, not wanting to be with her, not wanting to hold her and kiss her, to have his hands all over her, to pull her off to a private spot somewhere, anywhere, to make love to her before he exploded...

Lolly laughed as if she knew exactly how much he liked Paris. "I like her, too, if that counts for anything."

"It's always good to have your approval since you're a pretty good judge of character. Unless I'm mistaken, you didn't like Bettina, did you?"

"No, I didn't. But I think Paris might be a keeper. And if this baby is yours, well…"

"You're not going to give me a do-the-right-thing lecture, are you?" Ethan teased.

"I haven't had to do that since you swiped Old Man Nichols's boxer shorts off the line and ran them up the flagpole in front of the courthouse."

"Those were some *big* shorts."

"A 450-pound man couldn't get into small ones."

They both laughed at the memory, and Hannah joined in as if she shared the joke.

But Ethan didn't want to talk about doing the right thing. He didn't even know what the right thing was at this point. And he definitely didn't want to be thinking about the complications of this whole situation or how he felt about it all when he was headed for an evening alone with Paris.

So, before Lolly could go on with the conversation, he rubbed noses with Hannah and said, "I'd better hit the shower."

Lolly took the hint and reached for the baby. "Come on, little love, your daddy has to go."

"Shh! What if Paris heard *that?*" Ethan said, surprised by the note of panic in his own voice. The note that went with the slight ripple of panic that ran through him all of a sudden.

He handed Hannah over to Lolly and headed for the stairs, wondering as he did why Lolly's calling him daddy had rocked him so much.

Was it genuinely the idea of Paris overhearing it?

Or was it hearing it himself for the first time?

As if it were a reality….

* * *

"You know, there are a gazillion things I'm supposed to be checking on before the party tomorrow night. I really shouldn't be doing this instead—whatever this is we're doing," Paris said as Ethan drove into Dunbar at a little after five that afternoon.

"You'll have all day tomorrow. For now it's Friday night and you're off duty," Ethan insisted.

He pulled into a parking spot about halfway down the town's main street, and Paris glanced out her window to see where they were stopping.

They were in front of an old-fashioned storefront with Women's Apparel stenciled on both of the two huge cantilevered display windows on either side of a door that looked like the entrance to an English cottage.

That was when he said, "You have to have something special to wear to the party."

"Is that an invitation?" Paris asked, since Ethan hadn't yet extended one.

"I didn't know you needed an invitation. I thought it was assumed that you'd be going."

"Why would that be assumed? I'm here to be the preparations supervisor, remember? Not one of the guests."

"You're one of the guests, too," he confided with a warm whisper in her ear just before he got out of the SUV.

He'd come around to open her door for her before she could gather up her purse and do it herself. As she joined him on the sidewalk he said, "Lolly told me that when she unpacked for you she didn't see party clothes among your things. So we're here to get you some."

"Ah. And you don't have a doubt that I'm going to accept the invitation," she said, just to give him a hard time.

But he didn't take the bait.

"I wouldn't have it any other way," he said with confidence. Then he nodded toward the shop. "Marti Brock owns the store. She always orders in some fancy stuff especially for this. You should be able to find something you like."

"Is that her looking out the window?" Paris asked, referring to a very attractive redhead peeking over the pantsuit display with wide-set, exotic eyes that seemed to devour Ethan.

"That's her," he confirmed. And if he noticed the way the other woman was looking at him, he didn't show it.

But Paris couldn't help noticing. And thinking, Oh, no, not another one....

"Did you date her, too?" she asked as if she was joking when she didn't actually find any humor in once again being faced with someone who was attracted to him.

"No, I didn't date her, too. What do you think? That I cut a wide swath through the whole town?"

"Maybe," Paris admitted as she followed Ethan to the shop's entrance where he held that door open for her.

Through the introductions and Marti Brock showing her party clothes, Paris was grateful that the other woman wasn't as openly in pursuit of Ethan as

Honey Willis had been at the church dance. But despite the store owner's professional demeanor toward Paris, she still subtly flirted with Ethan. And when it came time for Paris to try on her selections, the store's proprietress left her to her own devices in the dressing room so she could hurry back out to Ethan.

It was better that way, Paris tried to convince herself. After all, she had to be very cost conscious and she didn't particularly want Marti Brock to know that the first thing she did before even putting something on was check the price tag.

But still she heard every one of Marti's lilting laughs from outside the dressing room. Every one of the other woman's coquettish comments. Every one of her veiled hints that she and Ethan should see more of each other while he was in Dunbar.

And because of that, Paris made quick work of choosing a dress.

Then she hurriedly slipped back into her black capri pants, shrugged on her white wrap blouse, crossing the two sides of it so she could tie the long ends into a bow at her left hip, and pulled on her sandals.

"That was fast," Marti said, not sounding pleased to see her again so soon when Paris came out of the dressing room.

"I found what I want," she answered simply and decisively, thinking that Marti Brock had found what she wanted, too, if the possessive hand she had on Ethan's arm was any indication.

"Don't we get to see a fashion show?" Ethan asked.

''You'll see what I picked tomorrow night.''

''And it's not the pink? I thought Ethan would really like the pink,'' Marti said with a combination of disappointment and disapproval.

''Not the pink.'' Definitely not the pink, which was an overly ruffled nightmare of a prom dress. Something she thought the other woman was very well aware of.

Paris stepped up to the counter to pay, and as Marti went behind to write up the receipt Ethan joined Paris.

''It's my treat,'' he informed her.

''No way,'' Paris answered without a moment's hesitation.

''Think of it as your bonus for a job well done,'' he insisted as Marti soaked in the exchange with open interest.

''No. You're overpaying me for this job as it is, and I won't accept more. Either I pay for this or I don't take it.''

''If she doesn't want you to pay for it, you shouldn't pay for it, Ethan,'' Marti said with enough double entendre to make Paris's blood boil.

Ethan ignored her and focused only on Paris. ''It's what I want to do. That's why I arranged for this today.''

''I was planning to get something new if I was invited to the party. So put your credit card away.''

''Paris—''

Paris cut him off with a shake of her head and handed her own credit card to the saleswoman.

Marti cast Ethan a sympathetic glance and reached

across the card he was still holding out to her, to take Paris's card instead.

"I think she has a mind of her own," the shop owner said to Ethan, making it sound like a negative.

But Paris didn't care at that point. She was too busy holding her breath in hopes that the sale didn't suck up what was left of her limit. If it did she thought she might have to commit hara-kiri right there.

But luckily the charge went through without a glitch as Ethan replaced his wallet in his back pocket.

"I didn't want you to have an expense over this," he said.

"It was a splurge," she assured him.

Marti chattered about how much she was looking forward to the party as she unceremoniously put Paris's purchase in a bag and handed it to her without actually looking at her.

Then Marti walked them to the door, saying to Ethan as she did, "I hope you'll save a few dances for me tomorrow night."

Ethan managed to laugh that off without promising anything as he held the door open for Paris.

And Paris was only too happy to step out of that shop.

"So, is there any single woman under fifty in this whole town who doesn't fall all over you?" she asked when she and Ethan were finally in the SUV again.

He laughed slightly, answering Marti Brock's wave goodbye with one of his own before pulling away from the curb.

"It's the money," he said bluntly then.

"What's the money?"

"The main source of my appeal. Marti Block wouldn't give me the time of day when we were growing up. It's only since I made a few bucks that she's discovered what a catch I am."

Paris glanced over at him. His hair was combed carelessly but neatly. His face was clean shaven, and each stark angle, each perfect feature, was in relief against the sun coming in through his window. He had on a black silk shirt with a band collar and a pair of black slacks that couldn't have fit him any better if they'd been made especially to his muscular specifications. And he smelled like heaven.

Somehow Paris doubted that his bank account had as much to do with his appeal to the single women of Dunbar as he might think.

"Maybe you just aged well," she suggested.

"Aged?" he repeated with a sideways glance of those blue eyes that could melt steel at a hundred paces. "You mean like cheese?"

"I mean like grew up. Maybe you were a gawky kid who grew up to be a more attractive man."

"I was a gawky kid," he agreed. Then, with a wickedly teasing smile, he said, "And now you think I'm an attractive man, huh?"

"I said maybe," she countered, rather than give him the satisfaction of a full-out compliment. "Or you could be right and it's just the money."

That made him laugh and change the subject. "Don't you want to know where we're going for dinner?"

"I didn't think there were too many options in Dunbar."

"We're not staying in Dunbar."

"Oh. Where are we going?"

"I'm not telling," he said like an ornery little boy. "I just wondered if you were curious."

"I am now."

"Too bad," he said, enjoying his joke. "Just sit back and enjoy the ride."

Then he slipped on a pair of very sexy sunglasses as if he were preparing himself for a speedway race, pushed a button on the CD player that surrounded them with Chris Isaak's music and hit the open road outside of Dunbar with a lead foot pressed to the gas pedal.

They drove for quite a while in the flat, open countryside of eastern Colorado. Paris kept watch for a restaurant, wondering if it was in the middle of nowhere or in another town.

Then Ethan turned off the main highway onto a two-lane road that ended several miles farther north. But not at a town or at a restaurant in the middle of nowhere. The road stopped at a lake where, at the end of a wooden dock that reached out into the water, was a very large boat.

"We're taking a boat to the restaurant?" Paris asked when he pulled to a halt, turned off the CD player and then the engine.

"Uh-uh. We're eating on the boat," he said as if he'd been bursting to tell her that all along.

Then he got out of the SUV and so did Paris, not

waiting for him to come around to open her door for her.

"Is this yours, too?" she asked over the hollow sound of their steps on the wood as they headed down the dock to where the *Great Escape* was anchored.

"It is," he answered, his affection for the boat ringing in his voice.

Someone had been there ahead of them because as they drew near Paris could see a table already set on the lower deck, complete with a white linen tablecloth, gold-rimmed china, polished silver and crystal goblets for the wine that was chilling in an ice bucket on a stand beside it all.

"Is this a yacht?" was Paris's next question as she took in the considerable size of the two-tiered craft.

"That sounds so pretentious," Ethan said with a proud smile. "You don't get seasick, do you?"

"I don't know. I've never been on a boat. Or a yacht."

"We won't go out too far. And if you start feeling queasy we'll come back and eat on shore instead."

"Okay. I'm game."

Ethan helped her board and left her to sit on the padded bench seat that ran in front of the railing that surrounded the lower deck. Then he climbed to the upper deck where a console full of buttons, levers and a steering wheel waited.

"Do you know what you're doing?" Paris called up to him.

"I've done it a million times before," he shouted over the loud roar of the engine as he started it.

He seemed intent on what he was doing so Paris didn't want to interrupt him and instead fell to just watching him.

He really did seem to be master of the vessel, but it wasn't his skill as captain of his ship that held her interest. It was the way his tight derriere looked in those black pants. And the narrowness of his waist just before it widened into the vee of his back. And shoulders so broad they looked as if they could belong to a swarthy, hard-bodied pirate manning an entirely different kind of ship....

"How're you doing?" Ethan asked, pulling her out of her study of him once he'd gone about half a mile from the dock and cut the engine so the peacefulness of the water could reign once more.

"I'm fine," she said, but her voice came out slightly weak because although she wasn't feeling any seasickness, she was in the throes of some internal rough waters caused by just the sight of him.

"Are you sure?" he persisted as he came down to the lower deck again.

Paris silently cleared her throat and, in a stronger tone, said, "I'm sure. It's nice out here."

"Isn't it?" he agreed with a satisfied glance around.

"Tell me about this boat," she urged him as he opened the wine and poured two glasses of the rosy liquor.

"It was the first thing I splurged on when I found myself in a position to splurge on anything," he began, warming to his subject as he came to hand her a glass and sit near her at the railing.

He went on to talk about learning to drive the boat and the fishing trips and water-skiing outings he and his brothers liked to take on it, regaling her with anecdotes of their adventures.

But Paris didn't hear much of what he was saying because as she sipped her wine she was lost in the moment itself and just being there with him.

The sun was beginning to set on the water. A gentle breeze cooled the hot summer air and gently rocked the boat. And Ethan's face was gilded in golden light that cast into relief the sharp planes of his cheeks, the chiseled blade of his jaw, the perfect patrician line of his nose.

And although Paris kept up her limited part of the conversation even through the cold supper they shared, she couldn't stop watching Ethan, studying him, being every bit as attracted to what she saw and heard as the other two women they'd encountered in the past twenty-four hours had been.

So attracted that as dusk fell and Ethan turned on the boat lights to cast a soft glow all around them, Paris began to worry that she was rapidly becoming even more susceptible to him than she'd been before. Especially when her thoughts began to turn to the hot kiss they'd shared the previous evening. To the way it had felt to be held in his arms. To wishing that was exactly what he'd do again right then and there.

Which was when she decided to guide the talk to something more serious to distract herself.

So as Ethan slid their dinner table and chairs out of the way while she went to sit again at the railing, she said, "Will you tell me now about the not-good woman in your life three years ago?"

"I didn't want to ruin our picnic with that. Why would I want to ruin tonight with it?"

"Because I want to know?" Paris said more flirtatiously than she'd intended. "And because I told you about my past. Doesn't that warrant you telling me about yours?"

Ethan again came to sit with her against the railing, only this time he sat closer than he had earlier. Close enough for his knee to brush her thigh when he sat sideways to face her. And just that small contact sent a heat wave through her that wasn't aided by the long arm he rested along the railing itself so that his hand was scant inches from touching her hair.

"It's an ugly story," he warned.

"All the more reason to hear it. The uglier the story, the greater the impact on you."

Ethan smiled a small smile. "Are you psychoanalyzing me?"

"Just curious about what makes you tick," she said, borrowing his reasoning of the previous evening.

Ethan didn't jump right into telling his tale, but she sensed that he was going to so she merely waited for him to start.

Her patience paid off a few minutes later.

"I told you Bettina came *into* my life three years ago," he finally said, addressing the wording of Paris's original question. "I was with her until just before I met you."

"Then it ended about the same time my relationship with Jason did," Paris said, getting the time frame straight in her mind.

"Actually it blew up in my face. But, yes, it must have been around the same time."

"And Bettina was her name?" Paris prompted when he stalled again, frowning out at the water.

"Bettina Gregory," he confirmed in a far-off tone.

"How did you meet her?"

"She worked for the interior designer I hired to furnish the house in Denver. She was a former model. Tall, beautiful, well dressed. Any man would have taken a second look."

He said that defensively and Paris didn't comment.

"We seemed to hit it off, so when the project was finished I asked her out. I fell for her fast and she made me think she was just as head over heels for me. We were engaged within six months."

Ethan looked at Paris again. "You're sure you want to hear the gory details?"

"Positive."

He stared at her for a moment, as if gauging whether or not he was going to go through with it.

Apparently he decided he was, because he said, "The first thing that happened was that her mother needed surgery the medical insurance wouldn't pay for. I only learned about it by overhearing a message on Bettina's answering machine and when I questioned her she reluctantly told me what was going on. She said she didn't want to bother me with it and I assured her that her family was my family and wrote a check to send to her mother."

"That was nice of you."

Ethan merely smiled again. This time wryly.

"Didn't her mother have the surgery?"

"Next up was Bettina's car," he said rather than answering Paris's question. "It was stolen. It was a pretty old car so she only carried liability on it."

"Which means it wasn't covered for theft."

Ethan let her know she was right by pointing a single index finger at her. "So I bought her a new car."

"Also a nice thing to do."

"I didn't do it to be nice. I figured we were getting married, my money was her money, why wouldn't we get her what she needed?"

That was a nice way to look at it, but Paris didn't say it since something about her telling him that seemed to aggravate him.

"Then," he continued, "her grandfather died. In Florida, which was where her mother had also had surgery—too far away for me to make a hospital visit or to get away for the funeral since he just happened to die when I was in the middle of a business mess I couldn't get away from."

"Just a coincidence?"

"Not quite but you're ruining my big climax."

"Never something I'd want to do," she said with a heavy dose of innuendo she surprised herself with.

But it helped lighten the tone slightly because Ethan smiled a genuine smile and said, "Good to know."

"Okay, so the grandfather died," Paris said to remind him where they were in the conversation.

"Uh-huh. Granddad died. Leaving a lot of debt and burial expenses the family couldn't pay."

"So you wrote another check. I'm beginning to see a pattern here."

"You're smarter than I am because I still wasn't."

"What finally opened your eyes?"

"About two months after the big death scene Bettina claimed she was getting squeezed out of her condominium."

"You weren't living together?"

"I wanted her to move in with me but she said it was bad luck, that everyone she knew who lived together before they got married never ended up getting married. What she wanted was for me to give her the money to buy the condo. She said the owner wanted to sell and she couldn't afford to buy the place. Or find another place within her price range to rent because the housing market in Colorado had skyrocketed."

"That's true. It's why my mother and I share a place."

"Yes, but Bettina and I had already been engaged for nearly a year by then. I didn't see why we should buy the condo when it was only a matter of time before we got married and she moved out of it, anyway. So that's what I told her."

"And she said…"

"She said the condo would be a good investment and we could rent it after we were married, that she didn't want to rush our marriage. And believe it or not, I was considering it. I wanted her to be happy. I didn't want her to feel as if we had to have a hurry-up wedding for any reason. But just before I wrote *that* check, I surprised her.''

''Why am I thinking it was you who got the real surprise?''

''Maybe you're psychic,'' he said, ''because it was definitely me who got the real surprise. I came home from a business trip two days early and went from the airport to her condominium without calling first.''

''Calling would have ruined the surprise.''

''Exactly. Well, *my* first surprise was that her stolen car was parked out front. But even then no red flags went up for me. I just figured the police had found it and returned it, and I let myself into the condo.''

''She wasn't alone,'' Paris said in a quiet, sympathetic voice.

''She was in bed. With her brother.''

''Her *brother?*''

''The man she had introduced to me as her brother when she'd talked me into paying his credit card debts so he wouldn't have to go bankrupt. In reality he wasn't her brother.''

Paris grimaced. ''That's awful.''

''To say the least. But thanks for not making any cracks about what a *close* family they were. I've heard more than my share of them.''

''What did she say?''

''She tried to lie her way out of it, but by then I was putting two and two together. It took some digging later on to prove it, but there hadn't been any surgery for her mother, her car had never been stolen, her grandfather had died ten years before I'd even met her, and she already owned the condominium. She was fleecing me, plain and simple. She and the boyfriend-slash-brother.''

''What did you do?''

''I learned more than I ever wanted to know about deceit and betrayal.''

That sounded uncomfortably pointed, and although Paris wasn't exactly sure why it should be, she wanted to get past it as quickly as she could. ''I meant did you get your money back.''

He shook his head. ''I didn't care about the money. I'd loved this woman and she'd just been playing me. That was the worst of it.''

''And it's why you're a little jaded about women wanting you only for your money,'' Paris surmised, referring to his comment after leaving Marti Brock's shop.

''I don't know that I'm 'jaded.' But I suppose I have been more on the lookout for honesty in people since then. And for ulterior motives.''

''And you didn't do anything to get back at this Bettina?''

''I thought about retribution at first. It was tempting, I won't deny it. I could have probably had her arrested. Or I could have sued her to get my money back. But once I'd cooled off and thought about it, I decided to chalk it up to experience and put it behind me.''

''You were embarrassed that you'd been duped,'' Paris guessed.

''No, I wasn't embarrassed. I didn't do anything anyone wouldn't have done for someone they thought they were going to spend the rest of their life with. I had the means and I'd trusted her and wanted to help her and her family. But if I had sunk to the level of prosecuting her or suing her... It just didn't sit well with me. In the first place it would have kept me connected to her—''

''Mmm. I began to wonder about that with Jason—whether part of the reason he kept at his wife and prolonged the divorce and even went after the kids was because it gave him a reason to stay connected to her.''

''Well, kids are a whole different thing. They're a part of you. They're your own flesh and blood. They're something worth fighting for if the need arises. But since money—and my pride—were the only real issues, I opted for swallowing the urge for revenge rather than keep in contact with Bettina even through lawyers or the legal system, and even if it meant getting my money back.''

''So that's what you meant last night when you said some people can take it on the chin and not try to destroy the person who hurt them.''

''That's what I meant,'' he said.

And for some reason her seeing that seemed to please him enough to elevate him from the darker mood that had descended over him as he'd talked about his past.

''Aren't you sorry you asked?'' he said with a charming, one-sided smile.

''No, I'm not. I'm glad to know.''

''But now that you do, can we drop it and go back to having a *good* time?''

It was Paris's turn to smile. "I've been having a good time all along."

"Is that so?" he said as if that, too, pleased him.

He took his hand away from the railing and toyed with a strand of her hair, letting it curl around his fingers. "Isn't it against the rules to admit it?" he asked.

"Are there rules?"

"You should know, you made them. I'm just a guy who looked up a girl he liked so he could get to know her."

"Are you sure that's an admission you want to make?" she teased him.

"That I like you? I thought it was pretty obvious."

"Or *you* just have an ulterior motive," she playfully accused.

"Like what?"

"Hmm. Let's see. You pick up a waitress at a business party and she ends up in bed with you, then you look her up again next time you're in town..."

He full-out grinned at her, and the crinkles at the corners of his blue eyes only made him all the more appealing. "You think I'm just angling for another night of wild passion?"

She arched her eyebrows in answer.

"Have I seemed disappointed that that's not where this has gone again?" he asked with a chuckle.

"You could just be hiding it well."

"And if an instant replay of fourteen months ago was what I was after wouldn't the 'strictly business' decree at the get-go have canceled this whole thing?"

"You probably just thought you could win me over."

Which wasn't too far from what he was doing as he let go of her hair and began a slow, featherlight massage with the backs of his fingers against her cheek.

"Is it working?" he asked in a confidential tone that made him lean slightly forward.

"I'm not going to sleep with you," she said with a smile, enjoying their game and the touch of his hand. Especially the touch of his hand as it traveled down the side of her neck and around so that his fingertips caressed her nape to continue that most tender of massages.

"Did I say anything about sleeping together? I wouldn't even if you asked," he joked in a low, intimate voice that only increased the heat wave that had begun when he'd joined her at the railing and his knee had brushed her thigh.

"Good, then we agree."

"Mmm," he muttered in a wry sort of moan.

But his eyes went on holding hers, and his hand at her neck went on doing that oh-so-sexy rub, and Paris knew something was going to happen. It had to. Maybe because she wanted it to so badly....

Then he raised his other hand to her cheek, laying his palm there a moment before that hand slid to cup her jaw and tilt her head as he closed the remaining distance between them to kiss her.

She didn't have any intention of letting him make love to her. But kissing him again? No real harm had come from that the past few nights, had it? In fact, at that moment it seemed as if it might actually help the craving that was coursing through her right then. Like one bite of chocolate cake on a diet to keep from feeling completely deprived.

His lips parted over hers and Paris's lips parted, too, as her hands raised to his chest almost on their own. To the solid wall of his pectorals.

Mouths opened wider and Ethan's tongue came to test the tips of her teeth, to find her tongue to torment, to tease, to tempt.

And it all seemed innocent enough.

It really did.

Until that internal heat wave started to grow in Paris. Until she found herself having to fight not to writhe with the awakening of every nerve in her body. Until her skin came alive with a driving need for his touch on more than her face, her neck. Until her nipples turned to stone and cried out for his attention. Until her craving turned into something more, something stronger, something all too demanding.

Their kiss deepened further still and Ethan wrapped an arm around her, pulling her closer to him. Close enough for her breasts to come into slight contact with him.

His shirt was thin and so was hers, and the little lace nothing of a bra she was wearing wasn't much of a barrier between them even though it felt like a brick wall keeping them apart. But still she wondered if he could feel the granite of her nipples, if he would know what was going on with her and if she should retreat enough to make sure he didn't figure it out so he wouldn't think he was being invited to do more than kiss her.

Except that she wanted so much for him to do more than kiss her....

As if Ethan knew she was contemplating moving away from him and he was determined not to let her, he brought her closer still, even as he abandoned her mouth to kiss a path to the hollow of her throat where the flick of his tongue left a dot of moisture to chill-dry in the cool night air and tighten her nipples even more.

Then he kissed a path that followed the deep vee of her wrap blouse. He kissed her collarbone. Her breast bone. He kissed the hint of cleavage that had somehow emerged from the loose blouse, and even though Paris knew she should push him away, she filled her hands with his broad shoulders, with the honed muscles of his expansive back instead.

His hand at the side of her neck went to tag along on the trail of those kisses, sliding down the slope of the blouse's edge as his mouth returned to hers with new urgency in the wide-open command of lips and tongue that Paris matched with equal vigor.

But he still only let his fingertips trace the edge of her shirt—up and down, up and down again—and regardless of what she knew she should or shouldn't be doing, she thought she might burst if he didn't actually come inside and relieve some of the burgeoning need to feel his touch.

Her back arched in silent message, and that seemed to be all the encouragement Ethan required to use the easy access the blouse allowed to finally reach one engorged orb.

And, oh, what a miraculous hand he had! Kneading with the perfect pressure, with the perfect contained power. Slipping under the bra to fit her bare breast to his palm, to let that striving, straining crest snuggle there as if it had found its home. Tantalizing it a moment later with fingertips that circled and gently pinched, that tugged and rolled and sent shards of glittering delight to rain down through her and ignite another need in that spot between her legs that she'd hoped would stay sleeping.

What had she thought before? That she didn't have any intention of letting him make love to her?

Maybe she'd been wrong....

But for some reason she didn't understand, right alongside the thoughts of how much she wanted him to make love to her came an echo of the things he'd told her earlier about his last relationship. About how he'd been deceived.

And even though she had no designs on his money, a stab of guilt over the deception she *was* perpetrating struck her.

And guilt for that suppressed her appetite enough to break away from his kiss with a renewed—if regrettable—will.

"We should stop," she said in a breathless whisper that didn't hold much force.

But even so it was enough for Ethan to heed, and he did as she'd ordered and stopped. Instantly.

He pulled his hand from her breast, out of her blouse, and rested it on her waist instead, closing his eyes and letting his head fall back as if searching for the strength to contain himself.

The water lapping at the boat was the only sound. Paris was still enveloped in the warmth of his body, and a thrumming need inside her made her silently beg him to overrule her veto. But he didn't. He stayed that way a moment longer and then he opened his eyes and dropped his chin enough to look into her face.

"I knew I shouldn't have brought those oysters," he said, making a joke in a deep, raspy voice that let her know he'd been as involved as she'd been.

"It's getting late, anyway," Paris said as if it mattered. "We should get back."

Still Ethan studied her and his eyes were filled with the same lingering hunger that was running rampant through her.

But then he smiled his concession, took his hand from her waist and his arm from around her, showing her both palms in surrender.

"Whatever you say," he said with a resigned sigh before he left to climb to the upper deck and restart the engine.

They didn't say much after Ethan had docked the boat and explained that he'd arranged for someone to come and clean up after them so they didn't have to.

They didn't say much on the drive back to his house or as he walked her inside, either.

But it wasn't as if there was a stony silence between them. For Paris's part, not talking was the only way she could hang on to that resolve that had kept her from actually making love with him. And since she didn't have a sense that there was more to it for Ethan, she assumed he was putting his efforts into the same thing.

But it didn't help when they reached her room and he took hold of her arms in a soft grip, sending all new bolts of lightning shooting through her.

"I really didn't mean to get you out on that boat to—"

"I know," she assured him.

"It's just that—"

Paris nodded because she knew without hearing the words what he was going to say—it was just that every time they were together something seemed to carry them away.

Which was exactly what was going to happen again if she didn't get into her room where she couldn't see his chiseled features and smell the scent of his aftershave and feel the magnetic attraction of his big body.

"We should just say good-night," she managed in a weak voice.

"And if I don't want to?"

"We should just say good-night."

He laughed a little wryly, a laugh that was more a rumble, deep in that chest she still wished she had her hands on.

"Good night," he said then, as if only obeying orders.

"See you tomorrow."

"Oh, yeah," he breathed.

Then he kneaded her arms just the way he'd

kneaded her breast only a short time before and leaned in to kiss her again, his mouth open and familiar over hers and very nearly costing her the tenuous hold she had on her self-control.

But in the end he didn't wait for her to put the brakes on a second time. He stopped the kiss as abruptly as he'd started it and let go of her, too.

"Good night," he repeated on another sigh, this one sounding full of frustration.

Then Paris ducked into her room before she lost all ability to go through with it.

But even long after she had looked in on Hannah, long after she had undressed and gone to bed, she still couldn't stop the burning desire she had for Ethan.

And for finishing what they'd started on that boat.

Or maybe what they'd started fourteen months before.

Chapter Eight

The last-minute preparations for the party made Saturday hectic for Paris. And since everyone in the household was just as busy as she was, there wasn't anyone to baby-sit Hannah, and Paris had to attend to most things with her daughter in tow.

That wouldn't have been too bad if Hannah would have been content in the stroller or the playpen. But the infant was having none of that. She was only happy perched on her mother's hip. Which meant that everything Paris had to do, she had to do one-handed.

By late in the afternoon, as Paris tried to make sure all the place settings were right, Hannah had finished her nap and was back with her. But the pure weight of even the small baby was beginning to wear on Paris and, when she tried for about the tenth time to put Hannah in her stroller, Hannah wailed as if she were being abused.

"Let me take her."

Paris hadn't seen Ethan since he'd left her at her bedroom door the night before, but she didn't need to turn around to know it was his voice coming from behind her.

"It's all right. She just wants to be part of all the activity," Paris said as she once more took Hannah out of the stroller and put her on her hip. Then she turned to face Ethan.

He was a little scruffy-looking, in sweatpants and a plain T-shirt that hugged his torso like a second skin. And for some reason he hadn't shaved, so his beard shadowed the lower portion of his face.

But even like that, one glance at him was enough to make Paris's pulse race almost as much as it had the previous evening on his boat, because his scruffy appearance only made him all the more appealing in a purely primitive, elemental way.

"Lolly says you've been carrying Hannah around all day. Let me give you a break," he said, holding out his hands to the baby.

Of course Hannah was delighted with the attention. She grinned and reached for him.

"See? She wants a change of venue," Ethan said, taking her from Paris to prop her on his hip instead.

"How about it, Miss Hannah? I have to talk to our bartender, want to come with me?" he said, nuzzling the baby's tiny button nose as he did.

And that was when, for the first time, Paris saw a resemblance between the two of them.

It was vague, but with Ethan's face right there beside Hannah's, Paris thought she could see him reflected in her daughter.

"No, that's okay," she said, feeling a wave of anxiousness as she held out her hands to take Hannah back.

But, as Ethan had said, Hannah was perfectly happy for the change of venue and ignored her mother to take a taste of Ethan's shoulder.

"Sorry, she's made her choice," he said with a laugh at what Hannah was doing. "She's decided to use me as a teething ring. So booze talk it is for this kid."

And with that he took Hannah to the bar, leaving Paris watching them with a fresh resurgence of uneasiness as she worried that it had suddenly become glaringly obvious that Ethan was Hannah's father.

But as she glanced around at Lolly and Aiden and Devon, at the rest of the staff all milling around, at Ethan talking to the bartender just the way he'd said he was going to, it was as if an earthquake had hit and Paris was the only one who felt it. No one else was so much as glancing at father or daughter. No one else was taking any notice of what Paris had just seen. From what she could tell, everyone was as oblivious to it as they'd been all along.

And that helped calm her. Not entirely. But enough to reason that if anyone else *had* noticed a resemblance between Hannah and Ethan, surely they would have commented on it.

So maybe she and Hannah were still safe, she told herself. For the moment, at any rate.

But one thing suddenly became perfectly clear and that was that she needed to get her daughter away from there as soon as possible. Before someone saw the two of them in just the right light, or at just the right angle the way she had, and *did* notice whatever small similarity there was.

Not that she could do anything at that moment. She had a job to do there, and Hannah couldn't be shut up alone in the bedroom while she did it. But luckily it was only a matter of hours before that job was finished. And when it was, Paris knew that she had to put things into motion to get herself and Hannah home.

Home, where they really would be safe. Where there would be no more reason to see Ethan again. Ever.

The champagne flowed like water, from a crystal fountain at a table in the center of the tent. Two giant pyramids of caviar stood sentry on silver pedestaled trays on either side of the fountain. More trays of hors d'oeuvres formed a circle around the champagne and caviar. And around that table were all the tables where the guests would sit when the time came for dinner to be served, each one clothed in white linen, set with china and silver, and adorned with a centerpiece of white roses.

All in all, it was an inviting sight as Paris entered the enormous, open-sided white tent where the party was being held. It was lit by tiny white lights strung in a glittering web overhead. Besides the center-pieces, there were flowers everywhere, scenting the air with their sweet smell. The violin quartet was playing classical music just loudly enough to be heard without making it difficult for anyone to talk. Guests mingled, full glasses in hand, carrying small plates laden with delectables, and from her vantage point Paris didn't see a single dour expression in the entire gathering.

But then, why would she when it was very much the spectacular affair Ethan had wanted it to be. And even though all the real work had been done before she'd come onto the scene, Paris was still proud of having played a last-minute role in it.

Lolly's niece was baby-sitting Hannah in Hannah's room, but the teenager had arrived late so Paris was making a tardy appearance. In fact, it seemed as if she were the only guest not already in attendance as she surveyed the crowd.

She'd considered not coming. Using the time while Ethan was hosting this party to pack her things and Hannah's, find a way to get to the bus station and leave before anyone had any more opportunity to see what she'd seen in Hannah today.

But Paris hadn't been able to make herself do it.

Not yet.

Hannah wouldn't be at the party, she'd reasoned. So if she swore to get her daughter out of there first thing in the morning, she thought she could allow herself these final few hours to attend the party she'd worked on. The party she'd looked forward to. She could allow herself this one last time with Ethan.

She spotted him then. He was across the tent, in a small group of men Paris didn't recognize. But one glance at him and everyone else seemed to drift into the background for her.

He looked much the way he had the night they'd met at the dinner in his honor fourteen months ago. Tall, straight, strong.

He was dressed in an impeccable black suit that had to have been specially made for him by an Italian hand. His shirt and tie were also black, he'd combed his hair more precisely than usual and shaved the day's scruffy beard. And if there was a more staggeringly gorgeous man there, Paris wasn't aware of him.

Then, as if her study of him had radioed her presence, he raised his chin, and his eyes met hers.

It was the stuff songs are made of.

Paris could almost feel his gaze on her and, without taking it from her, she saw him excuse himself so he could cut a path through his guests to come to her.

"Is this the dress you wouldn't let me buy?" he greeted when he reached her.

"It is."

He took her hand, held her arm in the air and made her twirl around so he could see it from every angle.

It was a fairly simple, silk chemise dress with free-form magenta-colored flowers printed on a background of cerulean blue. The blue of his eyes.

It had thin straps, and it dipped just to the initial hint of her cleavage in front and dropped low in back before it whispered down her body to her ankles where two-inch, high-heeled, open-toed mules were all she wore on her feet.

"Very nice," Ethan said when she faced him again.

His smile let her know he meant it.

"I like the curls, too," he added as he took in her hair.

Paris had curled it for the occasion, leaving it a springy, joyous mass that went well with the more dramatic evening makeup she'd applied.

"You don't look half-bad yourself," she countered.

"So I've been told by my two local predators," he confided with a nod over his shoulder at the guests in general.

"Honey Willis and Marti Brock," Paris guessed.

"Those are the ones. Which is why you'll have to stay close through this whole thing…to protect me."

"And here I thought you might just want my company."

"Oh, I definitely want your company," he said with a slow, lascivious smile.

Then he pulled her arm through his, closed his hand over hers to lock her in and said, "Let's go enjoy some of the fruits of your labors."

Their first stop was for champagne and caviar before Ethan began to make the rounds, introducing her to everyone she hadn't yet met until Paris gave up trying to remember names and just went with the flow.

As the evening truly got underway, Ethan made sure she never left his side, or at least never got farther than an arm's length away. They sat together at dinner, and when the orchestra began to play afterward, he danced only with her—to the chagrin of his other two admirers.

At midnight the party moved out of the tent onto the lawn for the fireworks.

It put to shame every Fourth of July display Paris had ever experienced as the night sky erupted with bright bursts of light that raised oohs and ahhs all around.

When it was over at one o'clock, about half the guests left while the other half went back to the tent where the orchestra struck up once more.

Ethan and Paris were among that half.

But by then Ethan seemed to have handed over all the hosting duties to his brothers, because his focus was so completely on Paris that no one even approached him any longer and they were left to just dance. Much the way they had at the church dinner.

Except that tonight, when Ethan held her in his arms, there was something different about it.

Their bodies seemed to fit together more seamlessly and there was an air of closeness that hadn't been between them that other night.

"So this is it. You're officially relieved of your duties," he said, his voice quiet, deep, sexy.

"I don't think I've ever been terminated quite like this," she joked.

"Not terminated. Just finished with your job. A job well done."

"You make it sound as if I did more than I did."

"You did enough to let me rest and relax more than I have any other year since we've been doing this party. I would never have been able to spend today playing racquetball with my brothers if not for your being here.''

''I guess that's something,'' she said, accepting his praise on those terms. ''And now it's back to the grindstone for you,'' she added.

''Mmm. I don't want to think about that right now.''

Neither did she, so she didn't say any more on the subject.

But even without any prompting Ethan said, ''I want to think about how great this is.''

''Dancing?''

He shook his head and squeezed her slightly. ''Having you right where you are. I'm glad I tracked you down.''

She had too many mixed feelings about his reappearance in her life to comment on that. Besides, her mixed feelings were what *she* didn't want to think about, so she just let him go unanswered.

If he noticed, he didn't remark on it.

Instead he angled his head so he could look into her face, into her eyes, and changed the subject. ''Can you feel it?''

For a split second Paris thought he might be asking her something inappropriate.

But then he explained. ''Whatever this is between us. It's like nothing I've ever felt before with anyone else.''

She knew what he was talking about but she only wished she *didn't* feel it. And rather than admit that, she said, ''Maybe it's the buzz from all the champagne…''

"Except that I've been feeling it even without the champagne. There's something about us together, Paris. About you..."

He let his voice drift off and merely smiled down at her to let her know that that "something" about her was something he liked. Something that intrigued him. Something special.

And that was how he made her feel—special, intriguing, appealing. It went to her head more than all the champagne had.

"We should just be enjoying the dancing," she advised him, because being in his arms was powerful enough. She didn't need the addition of words that were almost as powerful.

But then his eyes did the talking and they had no less impact on her as they searched hers, held hers and drew her in so completely she almost felt hypnotized by those absorbing blue depths.

Then he inclined his head just enough to kiss her. Lightly. Chastely. But it, too, had a power that left her weak-kneed.

"Behave yourself," she said when he ended the kiss.

But the command was as weak as her knees.

"No," he said simply enough. "I won't. I've been behaving myself all week."

"Do it for one more night," she said, not meaning for it to sound as beseeching as it had.

"No," he repeated, kissing her again. A sweet kiss that also managed to be so, so sexy that it chipped away at her resolve.

"I want tonight," he said then, forcefully.

It was her turn to say, "No."

But that, too, came out without volition.

"You don't want tonight?" he challenged. "You don't want just this one night like the one we had before?"

Before, when she'd given in to an attraction so intense it really had been like nothing she'd ever felt? Before, when she'd let herself get carried away and had a night she hadn't been able to forget no matter how hard she tried? A night when she really had been taken to another plane in space and time by this man who had given her the greatest gift? By this man who made her blood run faster just by looking at her? Who could elicit a response from her body as if it had a mind of its own? Who hadn't left her thoughts in the past fourteen months? Or her dreams in all the nights since he'd walked back into her life?

Did she want this one night with him before she had to make sure there would never be another?

She did. Heaven help her, she did.

She wanted this night. And she wanted him.

"We shouldn't," she said, anyway. But it sounded more like a confirmation than a refusal.

"Yes, we should," he said, kissing her neck, touching the tip of his tongue to her skin to tantalize her.

"Ethan…" she said, mentally begging him not to entice her.

But he just raised up to look into her eyes and smile again, that smile full of charm and mischief and a devilish streak he didn't usually let show.

"I know," he said. "I can come up with half a

dozen reasons why I shouldn't do this. But tonight is a night like no other, Paris. Let's treat it that way. Let me make love to you before I go out of my mind thinking about it.''

She closed her eyes and reminded herself of all the reasons why she shouldn't. Why she couldn't.

But it didn't make any difference.

He was right—tonight was a night like no other. A night that would never come again. And coursing through every inch of her was the desire to just give in to what she wanted, too.

To give in to wanting him.

To wanting him to make love to her just once more....

She opened her eyes to him, struck anew by how masculinely beautiful he was. ''Not all your guests are gone,'' she said, managing to hedge just a little.

''I don't care.''

''And we're just going to slip out together?''

''And we're just going to slip out together. All you have to do is say yes.''

He kissed her neck again, sending electrical shocks all through her before he nipped at her earlobe and, in a deep whiskey voice for her alone, said, ''So say yes.''

Paris closed her eyes again, and once more tried to resist. To resist him. To resist what she was craving.

But even as she did she heard herself say, ''Yes.''

''Oh, yes,'' he said, holding her tightly enough suddenly for her to feel the hard ridge of desire that was hiding behind his suit coat.

Then he stopped dancing and without another word, he took her hand and led her out of the tent, across the yard and into the rear of the house, not stopping to say anything to anyone as he ushered her straight upstairs.

"Yours or mine?" he asked when they reached the facing door of their bedrooms.

Paris hesitated. It wasn't that she didn't know which room they should use, she was just suddenly unsure if she should go through with this at all.

It wasn't too late, she told herself. She could put a stop to this before it went any further. She could say she'd changed her mind and leave him right there exactly the way she had so many nights this week.

But in the end she couldn't.

She couldn't take her hand out of the big, warm cocoon of his and walk away from him. She couldn't deny everything that was awake and alive within her. She couldn't keep herself from wanting him more than she wanted to breathe....

So she said, "Yours," knowing the baby monitor was in his breast pocket where he'd put it when the baby-sitter had brought it to them before she'd left at midnight. Knowing that she would still be able to hear Hannah from across the hall.

Ethan didn't question the choice, he just opened the door and took her into the lush inner sanctum of chocolate brown where a bed the size of Texas waited on a platform that was a step higher than the rest of a room the size of her whole house.

Something about that bed gave Paris another pause

as Ethan led her to its side and placed the baby monitor on the carved mahogany night stand.

"I hope I don't regret this," she said to herself.

"Did you regret it fourteen months ago?" he asked as he pulled her into his arms.

"No," she answered honestly. And she hadn't. Not for a single second.

That made him grin as he captured her mouth with his in a kiss that bypassed the sweet, chaste beginnings on the dance floor to seize the moment with a passion that seemed to have been waiting just beneath the surface to sweep her away.

And sweep her away it did.

So much so that she barely noticed that he shrugged out of his suit coat, that he got rid of his tie, that he kicked off his shoes.

So much so that she kicked off her own shoes without more than a passing thought as she wrapped her arms around shoulders she could barely span.

He deepened the kiss, sending his tongue to meet hers, to play, to tease, to torment as his hands did an arousing massage of her back where her dress left it bare.

Of course as they'd danced he'd laid his palm to her exposed back, but there was something far more sensual, far more intimate about his touch now. It made her want that same connection with him, so she pulled his shirttails from his slacks to slip her hands underneath it to the satin-over-steel skin of his bare back.

He aided the cause by unbuttoning his shirt and getting out of it, tossing it aside without ever suspending the kiss that was increasingly more open-mouthed.

Paris let her hands do some traveling then, around to his front, to the massive pectorals where male nubs were almost as hard as her own nipples were.

And her own nipples were definitely hard. Kerneled crests that strained for him, that cried out for the touch they hadn't had enough of the night before.

Ethan abandoned her mouth to kiss his way down the side of her neck to her shoulder as he raised a single index finger to the thin strap of her dress and pulled it down to her arm.

Then he returned to her mouth, not kissing her but sending only his tongue to trace the inner edge of her lips as he dropped the strap from her other shoulder, too.

The dress was loose-fitting enough so that without the straps to hold it up it slipped low on her breasts, low enough to brush the highest curve of nipples that were knotted even tighter now than a moment earlier.

Ethan went on kissing her. Her shoulder. Her collarbone, then the upper swell of each breast.

It took her breath away with desire for more. For his hands, for his mouth, on those engorged mounds of flesh that impatiently awaited their turn for his attention.

And then that was what she got as he covered one breast outside her dress at the same time he eased the dress down far enough over the other to free it to his seeking mouth.

She didn't mean to moan, but she couldn't help it

as desire—pulsating and demanding—washed through her, making her want him all the more.

As he kneaded one breast and worked magic with his mouth on the other, she let her hands descend from his pectorals to his flat stomach, to the waistband of his slacks where she unfastened them to drive him just a little crazy, too.

It must have worked because he groaned and used his free hand to shed what remained of his clothes.

Then with only his hands on her breasts, he reclaimed her mouth with his in a hot, wet, sexy kiss that was more tongue play than anything. Tongue play that was a sneak preview of what was to come, as he thrust into her, pulled out and thrust again.

But apparently there was a hint she missed in that, because a moment later he took one of her hands from where it rested at his waist and pushed it down so that she could close it over the burgeoning proof of how much he wanted her.

Long, thick, sleek proof that lit Paris on fire at that first touch and made him draw in a quick, deep breath of his own.

Oh, he was an amazing man!

And Paris relearned just how amazing.

It didn't take much for him to slip her dress the rest of the way off, leaving her in just the lace garter belt she preferred over the strangulation of pantyhose and the dark stockings it held up.

He didn't know, though, what he'd happened upon until he looked and then his second groan was even throatier than his first.

"Ohhh...that stays on," he nearly growled as he

scooped her up into his arms and swung her onto the mattress.

In the moment before he joined her, she got to see him fully naked and gilded by the soft lights from behind the bed. And if he was amazing to feel, he was more amazing to look at.

His body was even more incredible than she'd re-called in fourteen months of fantasies. Sculpted mus-cles rippled beneath firm flesh she ached to have pressed against her.

Then he was with her, lying beside her, half of him covering half of her.

He kissed her again—short, gentle kisses as if they hadn't already been plundering each other with aban-don.

But that only lasted a moment before he deserted her to draw one finger along her jawbone, following it with his mouth, kissing the spot just below her ear, flicking his tongue there, too, and leaving it to air dry as he kissed his way down the side of her neck to the hollow of her throat. He played there without touching her anywhere else, torturing her with the lack of contact her breasts, her whole body was crav-ing.

Then he came back to kiss her yet again, his mouth open and seeking as his fingertips trailed farther down, following the outer curve of her breast, barely brushing her nipple with his thumb, just enough to make it stand tall before his other fingers teased the tip with strokes so light they wouldn't have disturbed the petals of the most delicate flowers.

Up and around the entire globe of her breast those

fingertips went like the strokes of a sable paintbrush, then down her side, holding her in place as he kissed a similar path that brought his mouth where his hand had been.

Kisses, soft, sensual kisses. He circled her nipple with them, then traced it with the tip of his nose before taking it into his mouth.

The man had a wicked tongue that tormented the hardened crest, tugging at it until he'd set so many things alive in her that her spine arched and thrust more of her into the warm velvet of his mouth.

But he didn't stay there long.

Instead he placed slow, intentional kisses in a line to her navel, then down a bit farther to the waistband of the garter belt where his tongue followed the lacy edge, while his hand went lower still and found that spot between her legs that had come awake with a jolt.

Her back arched a second time as he slipped a finger inside her, then two, nearly driving her to the brink. So nearly that her hips writhed beneath his touch, flexing upward, inviting more.

He finally accepted the invitation, fitting himself between her open thighs, replacing his probing fingers with something so much bigger, so much harder, so much better.

And Paris was ready for it all. She wanted it all.

His mouth found hers again, demanding, his tongue delving in just the way that other part of his body was delving into her.

Deeply into her. Again and again. Striving. Straining.

They worked together on a wild ride that left behind all reason, all rationale, all thought but to reach that climax that awaited them both. That climax that took hold of each of them at once, that swept them into the vortex of pure and utter ecstasy. That held them suspended for breathless moments, frozen together, clinging to each other.

And when passion had spent itself and them, it eased them back—slowly, slowly—to satiated, heart-pounding exhaustion.

Neither of them said anything. Only their bodies spoke as he held her tightly and rolled onto his back, bringing her to lie atop him where he flung the edge of the quilt over her and she settled her head on his chest.

Paris was too exhausted to even think. About the next minute or the next hour or the next day. About anything but how incredibly perfect, how incredibly complete, she felt.

And so she allowed herself to just be carried toward the heaviness of sleep.

With Ethan still a part of her.

Chapter Nine

Ethan woke up at dawn the next morning but not without some help.

He was spooned around Paris, where she slept with her little rear end pushed into his lap, arousing him even in his sleep. And from the baby monitor on the night table there also came the soft, sweet sounds of Hannah.

He stayed right where he was, drifting half in and half out of sleep, absorbing it all.

Paris snuggled up against him.

Hannah cooing and chattering just across the hall.

It was a good way to wake up.

A great way to wake up.

In fact, even though he didn't consider himself to be an intuitive person, as he came fully awake he had the strongest, clearest sense that that was exactly how things were supposed to be.

Him and Paris and Hannah.

He opened his eyes and reached for the monitor, turning down the volume slightly so it wouldn't wake Paris, and then replacing it on the nightstand. But he could still hear Hannah's waking sounds, and it was so damn cute it made him smile a bleary smile as he settled his arm around her mother again.

Was Hannah his? he couldn't help wondering, even then as the wheels of his mind started up.

He thought she was. No, he couldn't be absolutely positive, but he definitely thought she was.

And he suddenly surprised himself by hoping she was.

Was he actually doing that? *Hoping* Hannah was his?

He was. Strange as that seemed.

One thing was for sure, it had sneaked up on him.

If someone had told him two weeks earlier that in only that short time he'd find himself wanting to be a father, he would have laughed in their face. He would have said he wasn't anywhere near ready for that. Maybe someday. But not right now.

But it was as if everything had been turned upside down for him just since walking into Paris's house a week ago, and the more he'd been around the baby, the more he'd watched her and carried her and played with her, the more he'd enjoyed her, the more he'd felt connected to her.

That was weird, but it was there inside him as much as the sense that she was supposed to be a part of his life, as much as the hope that she was his child. An intangible connection to Hannah.

Maybe it didn't prove anything. Maybe it didn't make it any more likely that she was his. But it wasn't something he could ignore, either.

Any more than he could ignore the fact that it wasn't only Hannah he felt connected to. The fact that he felt a connection to Paris, too.

But as he thought about that he began to realize that that wasn't all he felt for Paris. That there was more he felt, too.

In fact, it occurred to him that even if there wasn't a baby, he'd be lying there feeling that this was how things were supposed to be for him. That Paris was the woman he was meant to be with.

It seemed like something he'd known somewhere deep inside since the first time he'd set eyes on her. Something that had just been there, waiting for him to discover it.

And really, now that he had, he wondered how he could ever have overlooked it.

After all, the very thought of Paris turned his blood to molten lava. The simple sight of her was enough to stop him in his tracks, to make him forget about everything else.

How could he have missed the fact that she was the woman for him when he wanted to be with her every minute of every day and night? When he only felt completely himself when they were together? When the world only seemed full and colorful and worth being a part of when he was with her?

How could she not be the woman for him when

making love to her was like nothing he'd ever experienced before? When just the idea of making love to anyone *but* her turned him off? When all he could think about was being able to make love to her for the rest of his life?

For the rest of his life?

That gave him pause.

The last time he'd thought in terms of the rest of his life it had been over Bettina.

Bettina who had lied to him. Who had deceived him. Who had made him swear to himself that he would never get involved with another woman who wasn't totally open and honest with him....

Open and honest.

That was something Paris hadn't been with him. Not if Hannah really *was* his and Paris was keeping it from him.

It was easy to lose sight of that sometimes. It was easy to get caught up in his attraction to her, in these feelings that had somehow grown even though he'd tried to suppress them, in his feelings for Hannah. It was easy to forget that Paris might be keeping an even bigger secret from him than Bettina ever had.

But somehow, as he lay there holding Paris as she slept with her hair curling against the pillow and her long eyelashes resting against her porcelain skin, he discovered himself having a difficult time putting the two women in the same category.

Why was that, if they'd both lied to him?

But he knew why when he compared the two.

There had been something cunning about Bettina. Something calculated. And that wasn't the case with

Paris. He truly didn't believe she was angling for anything by keeping the secret he thought she was keeping.

Certainly she wasn't working some kind of scam on him the way Bettina had. Yes, she'd accepted the job he'd pretty obviously trumped up for her so she could get a new car. But once she was here she actually *had* worked for it—something Bettina would never have done.

And that was the only thing Paris had accepted from him. She hadn't even let him buy her dress for the party.

That in itself was the complete opposite of what Bettina would have done. In Paris's position Bettina would have not only had him buy one dress, she'd have come out with half a dozen, plus everything to go with them. And rather than turn down an offer for him to pay for them so she could pay for them herself, Bettina would have *expected* him to foot the bill.

But then, in Paris's position Bettina would have been cashing in royally. More royally than she had. In fact, now that he thought about it, it was a wonder Bettina hadn't borrowed someone else's baby to pull a child-support scam on him, too.

But Paris didn't even seem to want *that* from him. Which, if Hannah was his, she had coming.

So maybe Hannah *wasn't* his...

It always came back to that. Square one.

Just then Hannah let out a fairly loud squeal, and Ethan glanced at the monitor as if he would be able to see her through it.

Which of course he couldn't. But still the squeal seemed more insistent than her other, sweeter sounds, and he thought it was probably what she did when she was growing bored with entertaining herself and wanted some attention.

But the squeal didn't wake Paris and he hated to be the one to disturb her. Especially since, after a brief nap after their first round of lovemaking, he'd roused her for a second and then a third round that he knew had worn her out.

Besides, in that moment of wondering all over again if Hannah really was his, he wanted to see the baby. To once more judge if he was imagining things.

So he slipped carefully out of bed, pulled on a pair of pajama bottoms he took from a dresser drawer, and silently left the room.

He didn't hear so much as a stirring coming from the rest of the house as he went into Hannah's bedroom. It made Hannah's second squeal seem all the louder as he crossed to her crib side.

"Good morning, Miss Hannah," he said quietly.

Hannah took one look at him and grinned that toothless grin, waving her arms and legs in excited pleasure at seeing him.

It was such a small thing, that innocent delight, but the fact that it came in response to him went a long way in turning him to jelly.

She had to be his, he thought. Why else did she have such an overwhelming effect on him? No other child he'd ever encountered had.

He leaned one forearm on the crib rail and let her

take hold of the index finger of his other hand, searching her adorable face as he did.

And again he could see his mother in Hannah's eyes, in her dimple.

She had to be his....

"So why doesn't your mom want me to know?" he asked, as if Hannah might have the answer. "Is it what I thought that night she told me about that other guy? Is she just afraid?"

He considered that, thinking about the night she'd told him about her former fiancé and how he'd so doggedly gone after custody of his children purely out of spite.

But Ethan had tried to let her know that night— and the next when he'd told her about Bettina and taking what she'd done to him on the chin—that she didn't have anything to be afraid of from him.

Had she not gotten the message? Had he not said it forcefully enough to convince her?

Or was she just so terrified of it that nothing, not even the child support she actually needed, was worth taking the risk?

It seemed possible to him. Paris loved Hannah, there was no question about that. She was devoted to her. She believed Hannah was the only child she would ever have. That made Hannah all the more precious to her. And if Paris thought there was any chance of ever losing Hannah the way that other woman had lost her kids?

He could understand Paris keeping his paternity a secret from him.

But if that was the case, then all he had to do was put her fear to rest, he thought.

It seemed like an easy enough fix.

And if he did that? he asked himself as Hannah played with his finger. If he alleviated Paris's fears and she admitted Hannah was his daughter, what then?

Then they could be together. The three of them.

And that, he realized, brought him back to square one on that count, too.

But no matter how he came to it, he knew as he stood there with Hannah and thought about Paris, that he genuinely did want the three of them to be together.

Hannah let out another squeal then, this one louder and more shrill than the other two, letting him know that what she wanted was to be picked up.

He reached into the crib and obliged her, feeling his heart swell as he settled her into the cradle of his arms.

What had Paris said the day they'd had their picnic? That she would consider marriage if she met the right guy?

When she'd said it he'd hated the image of her being with someone else, the image of someone else parenting Hannah.

And now he understood why.

It was because now he knew without a doubt that *he* was that "right guy."

And not only because he believed Hannah was his child.

More than that, it was because he suddenly knew that he *had* to be that right guy in Paris's life.

Because she was the right woman in his.

"So here's the plan," he told the tiny infant. "We'll change you into a dry diaper and then I'll take you over to my room where we'll get your mom up. And maybe once we do, we can straighten out a few things."

As if she understood exactly what he was saying, Hannah cooed her approval.

And as Ethan took her to the changing table all he could think was that he hoped her mom was as easy to convince.

It was Hannah's high-pitched screech coming through the baby monitor that woke Paris. She considered it the warning bell. It meant "Get in here soon or else."

But Paris was sooo tired....

She couldn't move. She couldn't open her eyes.

Maybe Hannah would go back to sleep....

But she knew better. She knew from many mornings of listening to the soft, happy chatter that preceded the squeal, that when her daughter escalated to that, her patience at being kept waiting was spent. So no matter how tired she was, Paris was sure she was going to have to get up.

She forced her eyes open to mere slits then, struggling against the heavy sleep that still wanted to pull her back into its grasp.

That was when she realized she wasn't in the room that had become familiar to her.

But where was she?

First morning light came through windows covered in sheer curtains. The walls were painted brown and trimmed in cream. And she was in a huge bed that seemed to sit up higher than the rest of the large oak furniture.

Ethan's room.

It came back to her then. The party. Dinner. Dancing. A lot of champagne. Coming here to make love. Three times...

Paris's eyes flew open with that, and she shot a glance to the rest of the bed, the rest of the room, looking for him.

But he wasn't there.

Not physically, anyway. But she could smell the scent that was his alone. On the sheets. In the air. On her. And she could feel the essence of him all around her, as if the room echoed with his presence in the calm, confident color of the walls, the solid strength of the decor.

It was enough to make her almost feel as if his big, warm body was still beside her, as if the imprint he'd left in the mattress held her as surely as his arms had.

Or maybe that was what she was still craving even after those three times.

Then she heard his voice, also coming through the baby monitor.

And in a flash she went from wishing he would walk out of the bathroom door and get back into bed with her, to feeling uneasy.

He was with Hannah again. Hannah, whom Paris

had had every intention of whisking away before Ethan got another look at her. Before he had the chance to see himself reflected in her the way Paris had the day before.

She had to get in there, she thought frantically. She had to put herself between Ethan and Hannah before it was too late.

Paris lunged out of the bed, only aware of her own nakedness when the cool morning air touched her skin and reminded her that even the garter belt and nylons had come off by the third time they'd made love.

But she was less concerned with what to wear than with getting to her daughter as quickly as possible, so she grabbed the first thing she could—the black dress shirt Ethan had worn the previous evening.

She threw it on, trying not to notice the even headier scent of his aftershave wafting from the folds of it as she buttoned it as fast as her fingers could manage.

Then, wearing only that and heedless of the size or the fact that the sleeves fell over her hands, she turned toward the door.

But she'd only taken two steps in that direction when it opened and in came Ethan, carrying Hannah on his hip, against the magnificence of his bare chest above a pair of pajama bottoms.

"There she is," he said to her daughter when he caught sight of Paris.

The room seemed suddenly warmer just because he'd come into it, but that wasn't something Paris wanted to think about.

She just wanted to get her hands on Hannah and head for the hills as fast as she could.

"I'm sorry if she woke you up," she said to hide her own alarm. "Here, let me take her and you can go back to bed."

But the step she took toward Ethan and Hannah was canceled out by Ethan moving farther away.

"We're fine. I'm not going back to bed," he said as he went to the bureau across the room.

He opened the top dresser drawer and took what appeared to be a picture frame from it. Then he turned and came to Paris, handing it to her. "I want you to see something."

But Paris didn't care what he wanted her to see. She just wanted her baby.

"She's chewing on your shoulder again."

And what an amazing shoulder it was!

But that, too, was something Paris knew she shouldn't be thinking about.

"You'll be drowning in drool in a minute. Let me take her," she repeated.

Still Ethan didn't give Hannah over, though. He offered only the silver picture frame. "I want you to look at this."

Paris finally accepted it because she didn't have a choice. And once she had, Ethan took Hannah over to the largest window on the outside wall, propping one hip on the window seat there.

To Paris it seemed far, far away, and her alarm at still not having Hannah grew.

But since looking at the picture was apparently the only way to satisfy him and possibly get her daughter back, Paris did as he'd told her twice now and glanced at it.

Inside the silver frame was a wedding picture. A color portrait that was dated by the groom's shaggy, hippielike hair and the clownishly large lapels on his tuxedo, and by the flower-child look of the bride.

But that was only Paris's first impression.

Her second look was closer. Particularly at the bride, who had strikingly familiar aquamarine eyes and a tiny dimple just above the corner of her mouth.

And although Paris was looking at a photograph of people she'd never met, it was like seeing what her daughter would look like all grown-up.

She didn't know what to say so she didn't say anything.

"Those are my parents," Ethan said pointedly then.

In that moment, looking at that picture of his mother, Paris knew that he suspected Hannah was his child. That he'd suspected it from the beginning. That her thinking that she and Hannah were in any way safe around him had been an illusion.

A rush of total panic ran through her and she didn't know what to do.

But she did know that to verify it now was to give up the ghost, and she just couldn't do that.

So, hanging on to the hope that she could still bluff her way out of this, she tried to keep outwardly calm.

"They were very attractive," she said, referring to his parents and fighting to sound normal, to say something anyone might.

But Ethan wasn't going to let her off the hook.

"I know Hannah is mine," he said, confirming her worst fears.

"No, she isn't," Paris said in a hurry, as if the idea were insane and she couldn't imagine why he'd come up with it. "I had Hannah through artificial insemination."

"Don't kid yourself, Paris. There was nothing artificial about that night we spent together fourteen months ago. Any more than there was anything artificial about last night."

Last night was yet another thing Paris didn't want to think about.

"Hannah is *not* yours," she insisted.

"She's the image of my mother."

"She's the image of *my* grandmother," Paris countered.

Ethan stared at her with those penetrating blue eyes, and all Paris could think was that she'd been out of her mind to come here in the first place. Out of her mind to bring Hannah. She'd walked right into a disaster and now she was going to have to do whatever it took to get them out of there.

Then Ethan must have decided to change his tack because after a moment of studying her, he said, "I think I know what has you so determined not to let me know Hannah is mine."

Every time he said Hannah was his the possessiveness in his tone sent a fresh wave of terror through Paris.

"She isn't," she had to say even though it didn't seem to matter.

"I know that having seen what your former fiancé

did to his ex-wife over their kids had a big impact on you," Ethan said, rather than argue the point again. "I think it had such a big impact on you that now you're scared that if you tell me the truth the same thing might happen to you. But it won't, Paris. It won't."

"She isn't yours," Paris repeated firmly.

Again he didn't acknowledge it. "I considered that you might not want to tell me because I'd made it so clear the night we met that I wasn't ready for marriage or kids or family ties. Hell, until this morning I wasn't sure myself that that had changed. But I woke up with you next to me, with Hannah making those cute little sounds she makes, and I knew right then that *everything* had changed. That I wanted the three of us to be together. That I had to claim Hannah."

Paris's heart leaped to her throat. He was *claiming* Hannah?

Very slowly, carefully enunciating each word, Paris said, "Hannah is not yours to claim."

"Come on, Paris. I can get a court to order blood and DNA tests if I have to, but you and I both know the truth."

This was getting worse and worse, and Paris's reaction to it must have been evident because he shook his head and used a more cajoling tone.

"Don't go all pale on me. I'm not that other guy and I'm not looking to hurt anybody—especially not you. I told you, I want the three of us to be together. I'm crazy about you. I'm crazy about Hannah. I want you *both* in my life."

"So you thought you'd threaten me?"

"I'm not threatening you."

"Court-ordered blood and DNA tests?" she repeated. "What is that but a threat?"

"I just want you to be straight with me."

Paris took several steps in his direction, holding out her hands to Hannah. "Give her to me."

He didn't move much, but he did lean back just slightly. Enough for Paris to get the message that he still wasn't going to let her have Hannah.

"Don't do this, Paris," he beseeched. "I had to work to separate you from Bettina, to figure out that even though I know you've been lying to me about Hannah, it wasn't the same as what Bettina did. Now you have to work to separate me from that other guy. You have to separate what's going on between us and what went on between him and his ex-wife. Please."

"Please give me my baby."

"And then what? Are you going to run as fast and far away from me as you can take her? Are you going to do everything you can to keep me from ever having anything to do with her? And in the process ruin what you and I have? What we *could* have? I don't want that. I want you. I want Hannah."

"You can't always have everything you want."

"Don't tell me it isn't what you want, too."

"What I want is my baby."

"Don't make this into something it isn't."

Don't, don't, don't…

It seemed to Paris that he was giving a lot of or-

ders, and with each one she could feel herself stiffen
more and more.

Maybe he saw that, too, because he pushed off the
windowsill then and came to stand in front of her,
lowering his voice so it was softer. "Take a deep
breath and a good long look at me," he said. "I'm
not a bad guy. I'm not mean or evil or vindictive.
I'm the guy you trusted enough to make love with
last night, remember? I'm the father of your baby.
There aren't ugly, hurtful, hateful things between us.
There are only good things. Think about that. Separate it from the other situation, the other people."

Paris did take a good long look at him. At that
face that was handsome enough to stop traffic. At
those bare shoulders where her daughter happily
teethed. At the broad, honed pectorals she herself had
used as a pillow. At the pure splendor of that tall,
lean body her own body still craved.

And she was tempted to let down her guard. To
do as he told her and separate him and this situation
from what she'd witnessed of Jason.

But as she looked at him she also saw the power
of him. The confidence. The sure and certain knowledge that he could get what he wanted. Whatever he
wanted. The same kind of power and confidence, the
same kind of sure and certain knowledge that Jason
had had. That Jason had used when his relationship
with his wife had soured.

And there Ethan was, with Hannah, holding on to
her rather than handing her over. Keeping her from
Paris even after Paris had asked for her.

It was just too glaring an example of what Paris feared most.

"Just give her to me," she said, not understanding where the tears that flooded her eyes had come from.

He hesitated another moment but he finally let her take Hannah. And once Paris had her daughter she clung to her, stepping away from Ethan.

"She isn't yours," she said more forcefully than any of the other times. "It's only a coincidence that her eyes are the same color as your mother's. That she has a dimple. Hannah is not your baby."

She could tell by his expression that he still didn't believe that, but he refrained from refuting it. Instead he said, "Okay. Then let's just talk about you and me."

"There's no you and me to talk about."

"Yes, there is. There's plenty of you and me to talk about. We didn't come together fourteen months ago and again last night because there's nothing between us. There's something incredible between us."

Paris shook her head in denial. "Two nights. They were just two nights. No big deal."

"They were two very big deals and you know it."

"All I know is that this is the end. You hired me to supervise the last-minute details of your party, which I did, and now that the party is over, so is the job and everything else."

He closed his eyes and shook his head. "Paris…" he said in frustration. "Don't do this."

But she had to do this. She had to get away from him any way she could, as fast as she could.

And so, before he had even opened his eyes again,

she slipped out of his room and made a beeline for her own, where she swore to herself that she and Hannah would be on the first bus out of there.

And that nothing and no one would stop them.

Chapter Ten

They were sitting on her front porch on Wednesday afternoon when Paris got home. Aiden and Devon. One as handsome as the other and both resembling Ethan enough to make her heart lurch.

But she tried not to show any reaction to them as she went up the walk.

"Hi," Devon said as she drew near and both men stood up from the wicker chairs they were waiting in.

"Hello," Paris answered with reserve. She wasn't happy to see them and she wouldn't pretend she was.

Aiden met her at the porch's top step. "Can I take some of this stuff for you?"

Paris had been commissioned to do a mural at the elementary school, which was where she was coming from. Since it was only a few blocks away she'd walked. But she'd walked carrying an oversize sketch pad, her palette, and her paints and brushes in a large tackle box.

"I'm fine," she told him, but Aiden took the tackle box anyway and Devon helped himself to the sketch book and palette.

"You have a smudge of blue on your nose," he pointed out as he did, smiling in a way that also reminded her of Ethan. As if she needed any more reminders of him.

Paris walked to her front door rather than go on looking at the brothers, leaving the smudge where it was in a show of defiance.

"Why are you guys here?" she asked unceremoniously as she held the door open for them and followed them into her living room. She might not have let them in except she knew that her mother had Hannah safely away at a friend's house.

"We came to take you to buy a new car," Devon answered once they'd both set her things down.

"No, thanks."

"Ethan said that was your agreement for the work you did on the party last week," Aiden said, as if he hadn't heard her.

"I don't care what he said or what our agreement was. I don't want anything from him but to be left alone." Alone to maybe, eventually, stop thinking about him every minute of every day the way she had since leaving Dunbar on Sunday morning.

"You can relax," Devon assured her. "We're not here to plead Ethan's case. He told us not to."

She didn't know why that disappointed her, but it did.

"Ethan doesn't have a case," she said.

"We all saw the same thing in Hannah that Ethan did, Paris," Aiden said then, quietly negating her denial and letting her know they were aware of what was going on.

Paris had felt like a fool for having believed Ethan had accepted her artificial insemination story. For having let Hannah anywhere near him. Now she felt like twice the fool for not having known what had clearly been common knowledge to everyone else.

It didn't help her mood.

And she had no intention of addressing Aiden's comment about Hannah.

Instead she said, "I'm not going with you to buy a car, so you can go on about your business."

They ignored her invitation for them to leave.

And then, as if there had also been a decision to ignore Ethan's request not to plead his case, Aiden said, "You know, Ethan only wants what's best for you and for Hannah. He'd never hurt either of you."

Too late, Paris thought.

But she didn't say it.

"It looked like you cared about him," Devon interjected, apparently opting for speaking up on his brother's behalf, too. "Was that just an act?"

Like Bettina—that seemed to be the unspoken finish to his question. And even though Paris didn't want to, she hated the idea of being put in the same class with the other woman.

"No, it wasn't an act," she admitted reluctantly.

"We know he cares about you," Aiden said. "Can't you just try to work things out?"

Paris's eyes suddenly filled with tears. Tears she should have run out of by then since she'd shed so many of them in the last few days.

But she fought to keep them from falling, turning her back on the brothers so they wouldn't see and going to stand behind one of the overstuffed chairs that was at some distance from them in a shadow of the room.

"No, we can't just work things out," she answered definitively.

"Look," Devon reasoned, "we know that Ethan's money and what it buys can be daunting. There's no denying that it allows him to make things happen or that it can give him an edge in certain circumstances. But the bottom line is that what he makes happen are only good things. He doesn't use it as a weapon and that's what's really important."

So he'd told them the whole story.

"That's true," Aiden confirmed before she could say anything. "Even now, he could have lawyers beating down your door and he isn't doing that. He's willing to lose you, to lose Hannah and any rights he has to her, rather than force an issue he knows scares you."

"But we don't want to see that happen—losing you and Hannah," Devon said.

"The thing is, Paris," Aiden continued, "we all have someone from our past who leaves a sore spot we try hard to protect. But if we don't put it in its place and just use it to learn from, if we use it to build a wall around us instead, it isn't a lesson any-more, it's a handicap.''

"Is that what you want?" Devon said, each of them picking up smoothly where the other left off. "Do you want to be handicapped by your past? Do you want Hannah to be handicapped by it, too? By not having the father she deserves?''

"Do you want Hannah to grow up seeing a mother who has to keep herself closed off to feel safe?''

"I don't have to keep myself closed off to feel safe,'' Paris said defensively, finally interrupting them.

"What do you call it?'' Aiden challenged.

She only wished she *had* kept herself closed off. Then she wouldn't be as miserable as she'd been since getting back to Denver.

But she didn't say that, either. She didn't say anything.

"You're missing out, Paris,'' Devon said then. "And you're forcing Hannah to miss out, too. Sure, Ethan is setting up a trust fund for her. Sure, he'll make sure she's well provided for. But she'll never know him. And that's lousy. For all of you. When the three of you could be a family if you'd just give it a chance.''

"Just think about it,'' Aiden urged.

They had apparently come to the end of their not pleading Ethan's case, because silence fell in the room and this time they let it stay for a long while before Aiden took a business card out of his pocket.

"This is the salesman at a car dealership near here. They carry most makes, so you'll have a wide selection. The salesman knows to arrange for you to have whatever you want. If you won't go with us, then at least go on your own.''

He set the business card on the coffee table in front of the couch.

Then he and Devon retraced their steps to the door.

But as Devon went out, Aiden paused to look back at her.

"Don't ruin this, Paris. Not for Hannah. Not for Ethan. And not for yourself. You really could have something great with him.''

Then Aiden went out, too, finally leaving Paris alone.

And that was when she wilted.

Damn all the Tarlingtons, she thought, hating that they could affect her so strongly.

She rounded the overstuffed chair and collapsed into it, thinking that it was a good thing Aiden and Devon *hadn't* come to plead Ethan's case. What would they have said if they had? As it was, they'd portrayed him as the martyred saint who was forgoing his rights to his daughter just so he wouldn't risk freaking Paris out.

But then, how else would they have portrayed Ethan? she reasoned. He was their brother, after all.

Of course it *was* something that Ethan wasn't pushing his paternity suspicions, Paris conceded. That he hadn't sent lawyers to demand medical tests to prove it. That he was letting her denial go unchallenged.

Maybe he had changed his mind back to what he'd said fourteen months ago and he didn't want a child.

But Paris didn't actually believe that. Not after seeing the way he'd held Hannah Sunday morning. Against his naked chest, letting her suck his bare shoulder.

No, what Ethan was doing—or *not* doing—wasn't because he didn't want Hannah. Paris had no doubt that it really was because of her. Because he knew that if he did anything to prove Hannah was his, Paris *would* freak out.

His brothers were right—that was quite a sacrifice. Quite an act of unselfishness.

And definitely *not* something Jason would ever have done.

But just because for the moment Ethan was doing something that Jason wouldn't ever have done didn't mean Paris could overlook the similarities between the two men. The things that made them dangerous—money and power. And what that money and power allowed them to do to other people's lives. People like Jason's ex-wife and kids, people like Dr. B.

Although, since she'd been home with her mother, Paris had been giving the situation with Dr. B. more thought.

Ethan *had* lied to the old man, and that smacked of Jason's manipulations. But she'd come to acknowledge that unlike what Jason had done, what Ethan had done had been in the doctor's best interest. That if she were facing the same situation with her mother, she wouldn't be above doing the same thing.

Which took some of the steam out of her criticism of Ethan. Not to mention that the scenario had never held the same kind of vindictiveness as Jason's actions against his wife.

But then, that was what Ethan had said when she'd told him about Jason in the first place. That there were vindictive personalities and nonvindictive personalities. That some people could take things on the chin. The way he had with Bettina.

Of course, now that Paris knew that Ethan had suspected Hannah was his child all along, she knew that his point had been that because he hadn't gone after revenge for what the other woman had done to him, Paris didn't need to worry that he would ever try to get custody of Hannah from her just out of spite, either.

And maybe it was true.

Or maybe she just hoped it was true because she was trying to talk herself into something.

But then how could she not be inclined to talk herself into something when she'd spent the past few days missing Ethan so much she ached inside? So much she couldn't eat or sleep? How could she not be inclined to talk herself into something when, now that she'd seen Ethan in Hannah, she couldn't stop seeing him in her every time she looked at her daughter? When she couldn't stop wishing he was there to see it, too?

And all of that could be soothed if only she could talk herself into believing she and Ethan really might have a future together.

But talking herself into something could be very unwise, she thought. Especially when it might mean underestimating Ethan or the impact even a suspicion of parenthood might have on him.

After all, what had happened between Ethan and Bettina was on a whole different level. Bettina had swindled him out of money. Money he had to spare.

But a child was something else entirely. A child was something to fight for—he'd said that himself.

Only he wasn't fighting for her, Paris reminded herself again.

He wasn't dragging Paris through courts. He wasn't trying to force anything...

"And I'm going in circles," she muttered to herself since she was back where she'd started in thinking about this whole thing.

But maybe there was something to just that. Maybe if she was going in circles about it she should give the beginning of that circle more merit.

After all, for the past fourteen months she'd been convinced that the safest route for her and Hannah was to stay away from Ethan because if he knew Hannah was his daughter, and if he and Paris had any involvement and that involvement ended, he could try to take Hannah away from her.

But what was that last week if not an involvement? An involvement that had ended?

Yet Ethan hadn't sent lawyers to beat down her door demanding anything of her.

And maybe that was a bigger deal than she was acknowledging.

Maybe it was proof of just how different Ethan actually was.

Was that possible? she asked herself, again trying

hard not to talk herself into anything, trying to take an objective look at the two men.

But there were differences, she realized when she compared them as people. As men.

Where Jason was selfish, Ethan was anything but. Where Jason was thoughtless and unfeeling, Ethan was thoughtful and compassionate. Where Jason expected to be catered to, Ethan took care of other people. Where Jason did use his wealth and power as a weapon, Ethan used it to help out.

And where Jason was vindictive, Ethan took it on the chin....

So maybe where Jason couldn't be trusted, Ethan could be....

She wanted to believe that. She wanted it badly.

Because somewhere in the past few days she'd also realized that her feelings for Ethan were very different from her feelings for Jason. They ran deeper. They were stronger.

Too deep, too strong to deny any longer.

Yes, she'd tried. She'd fought them harder than she'd ever fought anything in her life.

But it didn't matter. The feelings were there and there was nothing she could do about them.

Feelings that left her wanting Ethan, wanting to be with him, so much that it suddenly didn't seem as if she really had any choice but to trust him...any choice but to try to make things work between them.

Because if she didn't, if she went on doing what Aiden had said—if she went on handicapping herself with what had happened in the past—she was never going to have Ethan. Hannah was never going to have Ethan.

And that was a very high price to pay. Too high a price to pay. Especially for safety from a man she'd misjudged, a man she was coming to believe she could be safe with.

A man she just might not be happy without...

So Paris mentally took her fears and all her misjudgments, and set them aside.

It was surprisingly easier than she'd expected.

And once she'd done that, she felt free.

Free to go after her real heart's desire.

And that was Ethan.

Ethan, who, she hoped, would forgive her for having denied him all she'd denied him in the past fourteen months.

Ethan, who, she hoped, really had come to the point where he wanted a family....

Chapter Eleven

There were worse times Paris's car could have broken down than that night, just after dark, on her way to Ethan's Cherry Creek house.

But not many.

At least, not many Paris could think of as her car began to sputter its now-familiar sputter and she eased it off to the side of the road, shrieking, "No! No! No!" at the top of her lungs.

And then it died. Deader than a doornail.

"Don't do this to me," she said to the car as if it would help, turning the key in the ignition—off, then on again—pumping the gas and hoping it would surprise her and start.

It didn't.

It just sat there, giving her not so much as a click or a chug.

She tried the engine again and again, but it didn't make any difference. And she knew it wouldn't. When the car stalled, it stalled for good.

"So what now?" she asked herself on a disgusted and frustrated sigh.

She took a look around her, not reassured to find nothing but darkness and a lot of evergreen trees.

She'd made it into Cherry Hills Estates where she'd been with Ethan that first night fourteen months ago. But the area was heavily wooded, and since miles separated one mansion from the next, she wasn't sure how much farther Ethan's house—or any house—was.

She didn't have a cell phone to call for help, and that didn't leave her many options.

Either she got out and hiked and hoped she'd come to a house before too long, or she sat there and waited for someone to pass by.

Not what she'd expected to be doing when she'd decided to go looking for Ethan tonight.

But just then her decision was made for her.

A car marked Security Patrol pulled up alongside her.

The uniformed officer who got out was an older man who didn't look the slightest sympathetic as he came up to the passenger side and pointed to her window so she'd roll it down.

Paris scooted across the bench seat and obliged him.

"Somethin' wrong?" he asked in a way that sounded more like an accusation.

"My car's dead," she said. "I was on my way to Ethan Tarlington's house."

The man looked from her to the car's interior, then to the car's exterior, and she could tell he didn't believe her for a minute.

But he didn't say anything. Instead he moved out of earshot and used a cellular phone of his own, presumably to call Ethan.

It didn't help Paris's already-high level of anxiety to wonder if Ethan was even there, since she'd only assumed that if his brothers were in Denver, he would be, too, and that they'd all be at this house. It didn't help her already-high level of anxiety to wonder what his reaction would be if he was. Or to wonder if he'd just tell the security guard to call a tow truck and have her taken away.

The patrolman reappeared at her window without warning then, startling Paris and making her realize just how nervous she was.

"Mr. Tarlington says he'll be right down."

No clue in that as to whether Ethan was happy about it or not.

"He said he didn't need me to wait for him, but I will if you want me to," the officer offered, sounding less suspicious.

"No, thanks. I'll be fine."

The man nodded but didn't say anything else before returning to his car and driving off.

As Paris rolled the window up and slid back behind the steering wheel she almost wished she would have had him stay. Because once he was gone and she was alone in the dark again, her stress seemed to come alive with a new force.

This was hardly the way she'd envisioned Ethan setting eyes on her again. She'd hoped to make a grand entrance of some kind, in her black spandex micromini skirt and the silky black spaghetti-strapped tank top she'd worn over it. Her plan was to look so sexy he wouldn't be able to remember that a few days earlier she'd dumped him.

But now the element of surprise was completely ruined and she just felt like an idiot.

Headlights flashed up ahead just then, blinding her and causing her pulse to speed up.

But the car went right past.

Not Ethan.

Her heartbeat slowed back down to the nervous pounding it had been doing since she'd decided on this course of action.

Maybe he wouldn't come at all, she thought as more time went by. Maybe even though he'd told the security patrolman that he would, he wouldn't. Or maybe any minute the security officer would return at Ethan's request to have her towed out of there after all because once he'd had the chance to think about it he'd realized he *didn't* want anything to do with her.

And then what would she do? Go after him with a paternity suit just to get to see him again?

Headlights shone from a different direction than the last ones, abruptly cutting off her worrying and making her heart race once more.

Was this Ethan? Was this Ethan? Let it be Ethan....

The black Jaguar pulled to a stop on the opposite side of the road, and Paris's heart started beating so hard it was like jungle drums in her ears.

What if he'd sent one of his brothers rather than come himself?

It was too dark to tell who was driving the Jaguar until the engine was turned off and the driver's door opened.

But then, in the dome light, she saw him.

Ethan.

It was Ethan.

She realized she'd been holding her breath and she let it out. Taking in another deep one and releasing it slowly in an effort to calm herself down.

He looked incredible to her. As if he'd gotten even more handsome since she'd seen him last.

He was close shaven and his hair had that tousled look that was such a nice counterbalance to the innate dignity and confidence that seemed to radiate from him.

As he got out of the car she could see that he had on faded blue jeans and a bright red polo shirt, but the dome light wasn't bright enough for her to tell what his expression was, to let her know what might be going through his mind, if he was happy to see her or angry from Sunday or annoyed at having his evening interrupted.

Then he closed the car door, the light went out and she was just left guessing.

Guessing and listening to the almost panicked race of the blood through her veins.

Don't let me have blown this....

Ethan came around to her side and tapped on the window with the knuckle of an index finger.

Paris felt even more like an idiot for not having rolled the window down yet, but she'd been so lost in fretting that she hadn't thought about that.

Now she rolled it down in a hurry.

When she had, Ethan bent over, resting his forearms on the door's edge.

"*This* is your car?" he said by way of greeting, amazement tingeing his voice.

"This is my car," she confirmed, referring to the nearly twenty-year-old sedan that had been in the garage every other time they'd been together.

"It's a boat," he said. "An *old* boat."

"I know."

Ethan poked his chin toward the other side of the seat. "Move over," he ordered.

Paris slid across, farther than she'd gone to roll down the window for the security patrolman, and Ethan got in behind the wheel in her place.

"It won't start," she informed him.

But he had to see for himself.

And while he did, Paris watched him, feeling as if

she was all twisted up inside. Car trouble was *not* what she'd come to talk to him about.

"It'll have to be towed. When it does this there's no getting it started again," she told him in a quiet voice that she thought echoed with her insecurity about what she'd ventured out to do tonight.

After turning the key in the ignition a few times and getting no response, Ethan accepted that and gave up.

But rather than simply getting out of the car and suggesting they go back to his place to call a tow truck, he angled himself on the seat, stretched an arm across the back of it, and gave her a long look.

"So what brings you out here? Just passing by?"

It was obvious that wasn't the case. No one would just be passing by this remote section of Denver that was designed to be out of the way so that its wealthy residents weren't easily accessible.

"I came to talk to you," she admitted.

He nodded his head. "Talking is good," he said, this time sounding encouraging.

It helped.

"Do you want to talk here or go back to the house," he asked.

"Are your brothers at your house?"

"Yes. But in case you've forgotten, it's a big place. I think we could find a room where we could talk without them."

Still, this whole thing was awkward enough. The seclusion and privacy of the broken-down car suddenly seemed preferable to the thought of anyone else being around.

"We can talk here," she said.

"Okay."

But that was it. He was leaving the ball in her court.

Paris found it difficult to just jump in, though. Horrible fear had forced her to keep this secret. It was no simple matter to expose it now.

But she knew she had to.

So after a moment she screwed up her courage and said, "Hannah *is* yours."

"I know. That's what I told you Sunday morning."

"But I told you it wasn't true and it is. That's all I'm saying. And that you can have a blood test if you want to be absolutely sure, but—"

"I don't need a blood test to be absolutely sure."

There was something comforting in that and in his matter-of-fact handling of this whole thing that allowed Paris to go on.

"I'm sorry I couldn't admit it before. But to me, after Jason, just the idea of you being in the picture seemed like the threat of losing her and—"

"I know that, too, Paris," Ethan said gently, patiently.

"I didn't do it on purpose, though," she said then. "Get pregnant, I mean. I want you to know that, too. That night—"

"I know what that night was. I was there, remember? I did all the seducing."

It struck Paris all over again that Ethan really was different from Jason because even though Jason's children had been conceived during his marriage, he'd still ranted about how his ex-wife had trapped him into having them so she could take him to the cleaners for child support if the marriage ever ended.

And yet here was Ethan, who could well have suspected she'd had ulterior motives, not doubting her at all.

"Anything else you wanted to talk about?" Ethan said then, as if prompting her.

She wasn't too sure if she could just blurt out the rest so she said, "I haven't been very...upbeat in the last few days."

"Neither have I."

"I'm not sure exactly where you were headed with what you were saying Sunday morning, but—"

"I was saying that I want the three of us to be together."

"Well, that's what I want, too. Whatever that means."

Ethan finally cracked a smile. A slow grin. "It means that I'm in love with you and I want you to be my wife and I want us to raise our daughter together and dance at her wedding and baby-sit our grandchildren and die holding hands when we're a hundred and seven. Is that clear enough?"

"Pretty clear." Paris couldn't help smiling, too.

"Clear enough for an answer?"

"I want us to be together. To be a family, too. I

want Hannah to know you're her father and not miss out on that.''

''And…''

''And I'm in love with you, too.''

''Finally,'' he said as if it had been like pulling teeth to get it out of her. ''So the answer is…''

''The answer is yes, I would love to die holding hands with you at a hundred and seven.''

''And the rest of it?''

She pretended to have to consider that before she said, ''Okay, yes to the rest of it, too. But only because you have a great body. It doesn't have anything to do with your money. Or your mind,'' she teased.

''It isn't because of my money?'' he said, feigning shock. Then, more seriously, he said, ''I actually knew it wasn't for my money because if you were Bettina and my brothers had gone to give you carte blanche for car shopping today, you'd be driving a Rolls Royce by now. Not that this low-rider isn't nice…''

''No shocks,'' she informed him, explaining why the car sat so close to the ground.

''No shocks. Really…'' he said as if it intrigued him. ''Maybe we should test that out.''

Ethan eased across the seat, nearer to her, staring at her so intently that she thought she could feel his eyes on her. And letting her know that what he had on his mind, now that they'd put everything else behind them was not something they should do in public.

"What if the local watchdog comes back?" she asked as Ethan hooked a single finger under the strap of her tank top and pulled it from her shoulder.

"We'll have a lot of explaining to do," he said before he pressed his lips to that spot where her strap had been.

Paris glanced out the windshield, then out the rear window. "We really shouldn't."

Ethan kissed the hollow of her throat. "We really shouldn't have fourteen months ago, either. But look how great that turned out."

He kissed his way up her neck, and somehow her head fell back so he could go on kissing the underside of her chin.

"Besides," he said in a husky voice, "this works for teenagers. Who knows, it might work for us, too, and Hannah won't have to be an only child."

Paris laughed again, but this time it came out a sexy rumble.

Then Ethan took her mouth with his in a kiss that was full of urgency right from the start, and Paris decided in that instant that she didn't care where they were or who might happen by. That all she cared about was this man and what he could ignite in her just that quick. This man and the fact that he loved her, that he wanted her as much as she wanted him. In every way that she wanted him.

He tasted sweet, as his tongue came to romp with hers. His hands on her shoulders were warm and sensual, lighting her skin on fire with desire for more of his touch, as her nipples turned to tight, yearning knots, and all on its own her back arched to relay the message.

Ethan understood it, letting those wondrous hands glide down to her straining breasts.

But just as Paris was writhing beneath his fingers, headlights flooded the car.

Ethan abandoned her breasts, and they both turned from their kiss to see if they were about to be found out.

But the car turned off before it reached them and again Paris said, "We shouldn't..."

But Ethan wrapped one arm around her to pull her to him once more, recapturing her mouth with his and slipping his hand under her tank top to her bra-less, engorged breast.

And she was lost again as that fire that had coursed across her skin now came to life inside her, burning a path to that spot between her legs that cried out for him.

"This is so bad," she whispered when his mouth deserted hers to replace his hand at her breast, to take it fully into that hot, wet cove where his tongue went to work to drive her even more wild.

Wild enough to pull his shirt not only from his jeans, but to also unfasten those jeans and plunge inside to that indisputable proof that he was as on fire as she was.

It was as if they'd been starved for each other for far too long. For so long that they could only push clothes aside while mouths plundered and hands ravaged and somehow they defied those cramped quarters for their bodies to come together. For Ethan to find his home inside her in a burst of passion and the overwhelming need to be one. To soar to heights greater than any they'd reached before, until they were both suspended in that blissful, explosive moment that truly bound them in a way no mere words ever could.

And when it was over, when the stars and the moon and the sun had all been reached, and they clung to each other as they floated back down to earth, Ethan kissed her once again and said, "I love you, Paris."

"I love you, too," she could answer then without any qualms.

"And I think we'll keep this car in the garage just so every now and then we can do this in it."

Paris laughed. "But will it be as good without the threat of the security patrol hanging over our heads?"

"Oh, I think what we have will always be good, no matter what," he said, holding her close for another moment before the headlights flooded the car again and they waited to see if it was the security patrol about to discover them.

It wasn't, the car went past them, but it was enough to prompt them to sit up and make themselves presentable.

As they did, Paris kept looking at Ethan out of the

corner of her eye, marveling at how much her heart swelled with just the sight of him.

And she knew without a doubt that he was right, that what they had between them *would* always be good, no matter what.

Because how could it be anything else when she loved him as much as she did, when she knew he loved her just as much, and when they had Hannah to share.

* * * * *

Look for Victoria Pade's next
BABY TIMES THREE *title*,

MAYBE MY BABY,

*in January 2003,
only from Silhouette Special Edition.*

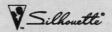

SPECIAL EDITION™

Coming in August 2002,
from Silhouette Special Edition and

CHRISTINE RIMMER,

the author who brought you the popular series

CONVENIENTLY YOURS,

brings her new series

THE SONS OF
CAITLIN
BRAVO

Starting with

HIS EXECUTIVE SWEETHEART
(SE #1485)...

One day she was the prim and proper executive assistant...
the next, Celia Tuttle fell hopelessly in love with her boss,
mogul Aaron Bravo, bachelor extraordinaire. It was clear he
was never going to return her feelings, so what was a girl to
do but get a makeover—and try to quit. Only suddenly,
was Aaron eyeing his assistant in a whole new light?

And coming in October 2002, MERCURY RISING,
also from Silhouette Special Edition.

**THE SONS OF CAITLIN BRAVO: Aaron, Cade and Will.
They thought no woman could tame them.
How wrong they were!**

Silhouette®
Where love comes alive™

EXPLORE THE POSSIBILITIES OF LIFE—AND LOVE—
IN THIS GROUNDBREAKING ANTHOLOGY!

Turning
Point

This is going to be our year.
Love, Your Secret Admirer

It was just a simple note, but for the three women
who received it, it has very different consequences....

For Kristie Samuels, a bouquet of roses on her desk can mean
only that her deadly admirer has gotten too close—and that
she needs to get even closer to protector Scott Wade,
in this provocative tale by **SHARON SALA**.

For Tia Kostas Hunter, her secret admirer seems a lot like the man
she once married—the man she *thought* she was getting a divorce
from!—in this emotional story by **PAULA DETMER RIGGS**.

For secretary Jamie Tyson, the mysterious gift means her romantic
dreams just might come true—and with the man she least
suspects—in this fun, sensuous story by **PEGGY MORELAND**.

Available this December at your favorite retail outlets!

Silhouette®
Where love comes alive™

Visit Silhouette at www.eHarlequin.com   PSTP

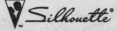

COMING NEXT MONTH

#1507 TALL, DARK AND IRRESISTIBLE—Joan Elliott Pickart
The Baby Bet: MacAllister's Gifts
From the moment they met, it was magic. But Ryan Sharpe and
Carolyn St. John were both scarred by a lifetime of hurts. Then the two
met an adorable little boy who desperately needed their help, and they
realized that having the courage to face the past was their only hope for
a future…together.

#1508 THE COWBOY'S CHRISTMAS MIRACLE—
Anne McAllister
Code of the West
Deck the halls with…romance? Widowed mom Erin Jones had loved
lone wolf cowboy Deke Malone years ago, but he'd only seen her as a
friend. Suddenly, the holidays brought her back into Deke's life…and
into his arms. Would the spirit of the season teach the independent-
minded Montana man that family was the best gift of all?

#1509 SCROOGE AND THE SINGLE GIRL—Christine Rimmer
The Sons of Caitlin Bravo
Bubbling bachelorette Jillian Diamond loved Christmas; legal eagle
Will Bravo hated all things ho-ho-ho. Then Will's matchmaking mom
tricked the two enemies-at-first-sight into being stuck together in an
isolated cabin during a blizzard! Could a snowbound Christmas turn
Will's bah-humbug into a declaration of love?

#1510 THE SUMMER HOUSE—
Susan Mallery and Teresa Southwick
2-in-1
Sun, sand and ocean. It was the perfect beach getaway, and best friends
Mandy Carter and Cassie Brightwell were determined to enjoy
it…alone. But summers could be full of surprises. Especially when
lovers, both old and new, showed up unexpectedly!

#1511 FAMILY PRACTICE—Judy Duarte
High-society surgeon Michael Harper was the complete opposite of
fun-loving cocktail waitress Kara Westin. Yet, despite their differences,
Michael couldn't help proposing marriage to help Kara gain custody of
two lovable tots. Would Michael's fortune and Kara's pride get in the
way of their happily-ever-after?

#1512 A SEASON TO BELIEVE—Elane Osborn
Jane Ashbury had been suffering from amnesia for over a year when a
Christmas tune jarred her back to reality. With so much still unknown,
private detective Matthew Sullivan was determined to help Jane piece
together the puzzle of her past. And when shocking secrets started to
surface, he offered her something better: a future filled with love!